Verse and Prose Anthology

Volume 20

www.lamda.ac.uk

www.nickhernbooks.co.uk

Verse and Prose Anthology: Volume 20

First published in 2024 by the London Academy of Music and Dramatic Art,
155 Talgarth Road, London W14 9DA, United Kingdom, Tel: +44 (0)208 834 0530,
www.lamda.ac.uk
and Nick Hern Books Limited, The Glasshouse, 49a Goldhawk Road, London W12 8QP,
United Kingdom, Tel: +44 (0)20 8749 4953, www.nickhernbooks.co.uk

A catalogue record for this book is available from the British Library.

Printed by TJ Books, Padstow, Cornwall
Design and layout by n9design.com

ISBN – PB: 978-1-83904-329-1
ISBN – EB: 978-1-78850-779-0

Contents

Foreword

There is a magic that occurs when words are spoken aloud, there is a music that fills that space between audience and performer that is punctuated by the words of the voice. It is a spell that begins with the writer but is only complete when you, the performer, share these words with an audience, when you share in the creation of an image, a sight, a scent or a sound that is birthed within the mind of the listener.

Approach this book with all the reverence you would for a true book of spells and know that you are one of the spell wielders, for the poems and prose contained within are seeds that you get to plant in fertile minds, it is no small thing. To run with the planting metaphor – a seed that isn't sown deep enough, or indeed too deep will not germinate, and likewise a performance of words that does not bridge that gap between stage and seat will not birth an experience in the listener's mind. So, take these words seriously, listen to them as you commit them to memory, let them sprout forth in your mind with all their fruits of emotion and truth so that you can pass that magic on.

Contained within you have the gift of the very best words by some incredible writers. Let the wonderful poetic silliness of Brian Moses intermingle with the power of John Agard, let the depth of Kate Wakeling's words intersperse with the glorious delights of Shakespeare and Ruth Awolola and Michael Rosen and C. S. Lewis. Become one with them, with me. As you read and then as you perform, bring us all together for that one timeless moment when there is an electricity dancing the auditorium, from our pens to your mouth to the listener's ears. Good luck.

Joseph Coelho
Children's Author
Waterstones Children's Laureate 2022-2024

Introduction

This anthology has been carefully selected to offer Learners a broad range of material when taking their LAMDA Examinations. Throughout the collection, we engage with contemporary writers who write for the modern world, whilst looking back to classical material from writers whose work has stood the test of time.

We also feature new, original material from writers who have a connection to LAMDA – including the winner and runners-up of LAMDA Learners' Poetry Prize 2023 – and it is a privilege to publish their work in this anthology. To LAMDA's Learners, we hope that this collection makes you excited to take your Examinations, whilst sparking your curiosity in different writers and the themes and topics they explore.

It is a pleasure to hand over to the likes of Bernardine Evaristo, Joseph Coelho, Louisa May Alcott and Oscar Wilde, and we hope you enjoy reading, studying and performing the works contained in this anthology.

Note on the Pieces

This anthology contains the set pieces for Learners taking LAMDA *Graded Examinations in Communication: Speaking Verse and Prose* from Entry Level to Grade 8, and LAMDA *Introductory Graded Examinations* from Stage 1 to Stage 3 (Solo and Group).

You may notice that in the case of certain selections, the spelling of some words may vary from piece to piece, representing either standard British or American spelling. To the best of our ability, LAMDA Examinations has selected pieces that are age-appropriate for Learners taking our Exams. However, some of the complete texts may contain themes, language or terminology that Learners may find offensive or unsettling. Please bear this in mind when teaching younger Learners, and note that LAMDA Examinations does not endorse any discriminatory terminology that appears.

LAMDA Examinations is constantly exploring ways to make our anthologies as inclusive as possible. We work with the industry to create positive change and encourage conversations around inclusivity. When selecting pieces for Learners, we recommend approaching this with sensitivity and consideration of the themes of the verse and prose selections, particularly in relation to religion, race, gender and disability.

Thanks

LAMDA Examinations would like to thank all the authors, translators, publishers and agents who made the development of this anthology possible. Special thanks are also due to Vinota Karunasaagarar, Stephen Mitchell, Githanda Githae, Karen Roberts, Oleksandra Spiegler, Andy Pitts, Linda Macrow, Marcia Carr, Simeilia Hodge-Dallaway and Beyond The Canon, Matt Applewhite and Nick Hern Books.

Solo Introductory: Stage 1

Flippin' Eck
Brian Bilston

This Speaker writes a poem using the method of making a pancake. Turn your book upside down to discover their recipe.

I wrote a pancake poem.
Instead of eggs I used some nouns,
poured in verbs in place of milk,
added adjectives for flour.
I whisked the words together,
cooked them until golden brown
then tossed my poem in the air.
It landed upside down.

I'm Nobody! Who are you?

Emily Dickinson

This Speaker considers what it is like to be an outsider.

I'm Nobody! Who are you?
Are you – Nobody – too?
Then there's a pair of us!
Don't tell! they'd advertise – you know!

How dreary – to be – Somebody!
How public – like a Frog –
To tell one's name – the livelong June –
To an admiring Bog!

From Aliens Stole My Underpants

Brian Moses

This poem explores the Speaker's relationship with aliens.

To understand the ways
of alien beings is hard,
and I've never worked it out
why they landed in my backyard.

And I've always wondered why
on their journey from the stars,
these aliens stole my underpants
and took them back to Mars.

Sugarcake Bubble

Grace Nichols

This poem describes the bubbling of a sugarcake.

Sugarcake, Sugarcake
Bubbling in a pot
Bubble, Bubble Sugarcake
Bubble thick and hot

Sugarcake, Sugarcake
Spice and coconut
Sweet and sticky
Brown and gooey

I could eat the lot.

Night Thoughts

Li Bai, translated by **Amy Lowell**

This poem portrays the Speaker's longing for home.

In front of my bed the moonlight is very bright.
I wonder if that can be frost on the floor?
I lift up my head and look at the full moon, the dazzling moon.
I drop my head, and think of the home of old days.

Hurt No Living Thing

Christina Rossetti

This poem communicates the importance of looking after all living creatures.

Hurt no living thing:
Ladybird, nor butterfly,
Nor moth with dusty wing,
Nor cricket chirping cheerily,
Nor grasshopper so light of leap,
Nor dancing gnat, nor beetle fat,
Nor harmless worms that creep.

Group Introductory: Stage 1

The Laugh
Joseph Coelho

This poem explores how infectious a laugh can be.

It started as a tickle
as a wriggle on my lips.
It turned into a giggle,
a wiggle of the hips.

It turned into a jitter,
a titter of the teeth.
My face is turning red
and it's begging for release.

It gasps into a guffaw!
Into a great big belly laugh.
If I whoop any louder
'Call the security staff!'

Now it's spreading to my friends
in snickers, chuckles and snorts.
If we roar any louder
we'll get a school report!

Now our sides our splitting!
We're on the floor laughing!

We cannot stop!
We will not stop!
It's threatening to choke!

And all because of the telling
of a wonderfully silly joke.

From I Am/I Say
Sabrina Mahfouz

This poem celebrates and protects the natural world.

We are part of the heart of the world
Don't break it
Don't break it.
We don't have the power to make it turn
But we have the power to learn.
Don't shake it
like a fizzy drink,
Too much up and down
Too much throwing around
The pressure mounts
The insides explode
Goes all over your clothes
No!
We all have the power to learn
To turn it all around
Care for the earth from below the ground
To the rumbles of clouds

I say
I say

I may be small
But I want more than sweets
Give me a world that beats
With the beauty it was given
Before any of us were living.

We are part of the heart of the world
Don't break it.

Jungle Noises
Nick Teed

This poem explores the sounds and noises of animals.

What's in the jungle?
Let's go explore!
Look, there's a tiger!
Roar!
Roar!
Roar!

What's in the jungle?
Let's take a peek!
Look, there's a jungle rat!
Squeak!
Squeak!
Squeak!

What's in the jungle?
Let's take a walk!
Look, there's a parrot!
Squawk!
Squawk!
Squawk!

What's in the jungle?
Let's look at this!
Look, there's a snake!
Hiss!
Hiss!
Hiss!

What's in the jungle?
No time to nap!
Look, there's a crocodile!
Snap!
Snap!
Snap!

It's great here in the jungle,
Bathed in the sun!
Seeing all the animals!
Fun!
Fun!
Fun!

Solo Introductory: Stage 2

There's a Shark in my Tea!

Leo Alderin (Runner-up in LAMDA Learners' Poetry Prize 2023)

This Speaker sees something suspicious in their cup of tea.

There's a shark in my tea!
How did it get in there?
It's bobbing up and down
Giving me quite a scare.

I'm so glad I saw it
Before I took a sip
Otherwise it might have tried
To bite me on my lip!

I can't believe my eyes
It is a great big fin...
Oh dear... I need to tell Mum
That she left the tea bag in!

Gibberish

Mary Elizabeth Coleridge

This is poem of nonsense, where birds blossom and flowers sing.

Many a flower have I seen blossom,
Many a bird for me will sing.
Never heard I so sweet a singer,
Never saw I so fair a thing.

She is a bird, a bird that blossoms,
She is a flower, a flower that sings;
And I a flower when I behold her,
And when I hear her, I have wings.

Cold Toast
Claudine Toutoungi

In this poem, the Speaker sends some toast in the post.

I made you some toast
It went in the post

I mailed it first class
with jam on one half

When it lands on your mat
it should be quite flat

if a little bit burnt
(though I scraped off the worst)

Cold toast it will be
but if you chew vigorously

and drink some hot tea
it will slip down wonderfully

The Storm
Sara Coleridge

This poem depicts a raging storm, before it clears into a brighter day.

See lightning is flashing,
The forest is crashing,
The rain will come dashing,
A flood will be rising anon;

The heavens are scowling,
The thunder is growling,
The loud winds are howling,
The storm has come suddenly on!

But now the sky clears,
The bright sun appears,
Now nobody fears,
But soon every cloud will be gone.

Let Thine Eyes Whisper

Ameen Rihani

This Speaker provides comfort to someone struggling with grief and regret.

Grieve not, for I am near thee;
  Sigh not, for I can hear thee;
Wash from thy heart all memory of past wrong;
   Doubt not that doubts besmear thee;
  Speak not, for I do fear thee;
Let thine eyes whisper love's conciling song.

Bird, Bell, and I

Misuzu Kaneko, translated by **Sally Ito** and **Michiko Tsuboi**

This poem celebrates difference and individuality.

Even if I spread my arms wide,
I can't fly through the sky,
but still the little bird who flies
can't run on the ground as fast as I.

Even if I shake my body about
no pretty sound comes out,
but still, the tinkling bell
doesn't know as many songs as I.

Bird, bell, and I,
We're all different, and that's just fine.

Group Introductory: Stage 2

Hopaloo Kangaroo

John Agard

This poem playfully describes the movement of a kangaroo.

If you can jigaloo
jigaloo
I can do the jigaloo too,
for I'm the jiggiest
jigaloo kangaroo

jigaloo all night through
jigaloo all night through

If you can boogaloo
boogaloo
I can do the boogaloo too
for I'm the boogiest
boogaloo kangaroo.

boogaloo all night through
boogaloo all night through

But bet you can't hopaloo
hopaloo
like I can do
for I'm the hoppiest
hopaloo kangaroo

hopaloo all night through
hopaloo all night through

Gonna show you steps
you never knew,
And guess what, guys?
My baby in my pouch
Will be dancing too.

The Last Shot

Kwame Alexander

In a competitive basketball game, the team take their last shot of the match.

They DOUBLE-team me
I'm in DOUBLE trouble
Trying not to DOUBLE dribble
Gotta get out the DOUBLE trap
So I *juke* one
But number two follows
So I *QUICKLY*
DOUBLE **cross** (*and it works*)
And he f

a

l

l

s   WHOOPS!

Hits the Splits,
I wanna shoot baaaaaaaaaaaad
But I. Don't. Know.
If. I. Can. Make. It.
If I can shake this
F E A R
Plus it's only
Seven seconds
On the clock
And if I miss it's
C L E A R
This. Game. Is. Over.
But if I s.c.o.r.e.
We win
And I'm the HERO!
(*Don't screw it up, Charlie*)
Roxie's at the free-throw line
(*I once saw her make like fifteen in a row*)

I **shoot** her
The **ball**
And it goes over
Her head almost, but
She snatches it
  Out the air
    Plants her feet
      On the line
        TOP of the key
       No one on her
        She's **FREE**
          Ready to SHINE
           Like she's a STAR
          Like she was made
         For this shot
          FOR THE LAST SHOT
         And she was
         And she is
          And she shoots
         And she

misses.

Wallaby Trouble

Monika Johnson

This poem follows the Speaker's relationship with their new pet: a naughty wallaby.

I had a brand-new wallaby
I got him from the zoo.
He just looked kind of lonely
with nothing much to do.

So, whilst my teacher and my mates
saw the big baboon,
I popped Wally in my lunchbox
between my yogurt and my spoon.

Wally liked adventures
he didn't miss the zoo.
I made him all domestic
like all good owners do.

On Monday we played football
we were winning 7-2
but then Wally jumped the goalposts
and gave the referee the boot!
Ouch.

Last Friday we went skating –
we whizzed past George and Lou!
Then Wally bounced and broke the ice
and soaked us all wet through!

I think having a pet wallaby
is harder than it looks.
They don't like eating pancakes
and they chew up my school books.

I know that I'll miss Wally
when he goes back to the zoo.
But wallabies aren't made for pets
So, I've got a kangaroo!

Solo Introductory: Stage 3

Dis Breeze
Valerie Bloom

This poem explores the mischievousness of a breeze.

Dis breeze is an air conditioner,
Dis breeze better than any fan,
Dis breeze blow soft an' warm
Dry me face an' foot an' han.

Dis breeze don't have no manners,
Dis breeze is much too bold,
Look how dis breeze lift up me skirt
And show me knickers to the world!

The Slime Takeover

Joseph Coelho

This poem explores the colour, texture and movement of slime.

Slipping, shimmering, stinking slime,
sloppy cerise or shades of scarlet sublime.
It sticks and sucks and spits and spools,
snaking slime slumping several school walls.
The slime swells, and stretches, and starts to sprout,
sliming several school halls as students scream and shout.
'Scary Slime Subsumes Schools',
say a slew of scandal sheets.
Their swan song headline
as the slime swallows scores of the city's streets.

Ariel's Song

William Shakespeare

This poem portrays the image of a man lying on the ocean floor.

Full fathom five thy father lies,
Of his bones are coral made;
Those are pearls that were his eyes,
Nothing of him that doth fade
But doth suffer a sea-change
Into something rich and strange.
Sea Nymphs hourly ring his knell.
Ding dong.
Hark, now I hear them.
Ding dong bell.

I am angry
Michael Rosen

This poem is an expression of the feeling of anger.

I am angry. really angry. angry,
angry, angry. I'm so angry
I'll jump up and down. I'll roll on the ground
Make a din. Make you spin
Pull out my hair. Throw you in the air
Pull down posts. Hunt down ghosts
Scare spiders. Scare tigers
Pull up trees. Bully bees
Rattle the radiators. Frighten alligators
Cut down flowers. Bring down towers
Bang all the bones. Wake up stones
Shake the tiles. Stop all smiles
Silence birds. Boil words
Mash up names. Grind up games
Crush tunes. Squash moons
Make giants run. Terrify the sun
Turn the sky red. And then go to bed.

From # The First Tooth

Mary and **Charles Lamb**

This poem explores an older sister's envy towards her little brother.

Through the house what busy joy
Just because the infant boy
Has a tiny tooth to show!
I have got a double row,
All as white and all as small;
Yet no one cares for mine at all.
He can say but half a word,
Yet that single sound's preferr'd
To all the words that I can say
In the longest summer day.
He cannot walk; yet if he put
With mimic motion out his foot,
As if he thought he were advancing,
It's prized more than my best dancing.

Bertie Beaky

Claudine Toutoungi

This poem depicts life with a pterodactyl in the kitchen.

The pterodactyl in my kitchen
– Mr Beaky, if you please –
likes to skim around the ceiling,
likes to share a plate of cheese.

Mr Beaky is quite something
(though he very rarely sings).
He can play the concertina
with his creased-up, crooked wings.

And he'll dive-bomb the recycling
to sort the plastic from the glass.
Mr Beaky is a marvel
of the very topmost class.

Group Introductory: Stage 3

The Both of Us

Joshua Seigal

This poem uses contrast to explore companionship and loneliness.

I used to be a butterfly
but now I'm just a slug.
I used to be a toothy grin
but now I'm just a shrug.
I used to be a rainforest
but now I'm just a tree.
It used to be the both of us
but now it's only me.

I used to be an estuary
but now I'm just a brook.
I used to be a library
but now I'm just a book.
I used to be a sanctuary
but now I'm just a zoo.
It used to be the both of us
but now there isn't you.

I used to be a dinosaur
but now I'm just a mouse.
I used to be a cityscape
but now I'm just a house.
I used to be a bakery
but now I'm just a bun.
It used to be the both of us
but now there's only one.

I used to be a symphony
but now I'm just a note.
I used to be democracy
but now I'm just a vote.
I used to be Mount Everest
but now I'm just a stone.
It used to be the both of us
but now I'm all alone.

The Flibbit

Kate Wakeling

This poem portrays the antics of a mischievous and mysterious flibbit.

Here's the thing about the flibbit,
as it's time someone explained:
she's quick as light and light as air,
with mischief on the brain.

When you're sitting somewhere solemn
and it's crucial you don't sneeze,
she's what tickles at your nostrils
(with her small and knobbly knees).

Or if you've put your shoes on
and are ready to step out
but find an itch between your toes,
well, reader, have no doubt:

it's the flibbit, yes the flibbit,
minor mayhem is her mission,
she's the overlord of awkward,
irritation's top magician.

That tingle on your scalp you get
when someone mentions nits?
Mull no more, for in your hair
a certain someone sits.

It's the flibbit, yes the flibbit,
who is fiddling with your follicles,
this flibbit loves the whipping up
of just such little obstacles.

She's Ninja of the Niggle,
the nano nag you can't ignore,
but take note: her naughty knack
is only nuisance, nothing more.

So if you find yourself in trouble
for a fretful sort of fidget,
remember just to answer:
NOT MY FAULT, IT WAS THE FLIBBIT.

The Months
Sara Coleridge

This poem presents a catalogue of the months of the year, each with unique qualities.

January brings the snow,
Makes our feet and fingers glow.

February brings the rain,
Thaws the frozen lake again.

March brings breezes loud and shrill,
Stirs the dancing daffodil.

April brings the primrose sweet,
Scatters daises at our feet.

May brings flocks of pretty lambs,
Skipping by their fleecy damns.

June brings tulips, lilies, roses,
Fills the children's hand with posies.

Hot July brings cooling showers,
Apricots and gilliflowers.

August brings the sheaves of corn,
Then the harvest home is borne.

Warm September brings the fruit,
Sportsmen then begin to shoot.

Fresh October brings the pheasant,
Then to gather nuts is pleasant.

Dull November brings the blast,
Then the leaves are whirling fast.

Chill December brings the sleet,
Blazing fire, and Christmas treat.

Entry Level Speaking Verse and Prose

The Shockadile Crocodile!

Joseph Coelho

This poem describes the Speaker's relationship with their best friend, a crocodile.

I have a snappy best friend
she is a croc-ODILE.
When I call for her I have to
knock-ODILE.
She lives on the third floor
of a block-ODILE.
>She loves loud music
>she likes to rock-ODILE.
>She's a great dancer
>she can pop and lock-ODILE.
>A super flashy dresser
>like a peacock-ODILE.
She has amazing patterns
on her sock-ODILES.
>She won't be caught dead wearing
>>a frock-ODILE.
>>She does what she wants
>she is a shock-ODILE.
My incredible best friend
  is a shock-ODILE,
frock-ODILE,
>sock-ODILE,
>>peacock-ODILE,
>lock-ODILE,
>>rock-ODILE,
>>>block-ODILE,
>>>knock-ODILE
>>>CROCODILE!

From the Arabic

Ameen Rihani

This poem explores love and heartbreak.

Why art thou so hushed and sad,
  So thin and wan?
Who robbed thee of thy flesh and song, –
  Was it Ramadhan?

Nay, Ramadhan is not to blame,
  For I have ceased to fast and pray;
But to my vacant Dwelling came
  An unknown Guest – he came to stay.

And in my heart he eats and drinks;
  He drinks my blood, of wines the best,
And eats my burning flesh, – ah, yes,
  My love for Zahra is that Guest.

Seasons
Valerie Bloom

This poem personifies the seasons to depict their unique qualities.

Spring is baby,
bright, fresh and new,
gurgling with the melting snow,
singing with the first cuckoo.
Summer is a barefoot boy,
fishing in the stream,
running through the waiting corn,
lazing in a dream.
Autumn's a grown man,
slowly walking by,
a limp in his careful footstep,
a shadow in one eye.
Winter is an aged sage,
with long, snow-powdered hair.
He cuts a trench in the frozen ground,
and buries another year.

Colour
Christina Rossetti

This poem uses questions and answers to describe different colours.

What is pink? a rose is pink
By the fountain's brink.
What is red? a poppy's red
In its barley bed.
What is blue? the sky is blue
Where the clouds float thro'.
What is white? a swan is white
Sailing in the light.
What is yellow? pears are yellow,
Rich and ripe and mellow.
What is green? the grass is green,
With small flowers between.
What is violet? clouds are violet
In the summer twilight.
What is orange? why, an orange,
Just an orange!

Chameleon Kids

Matt Goodfellow

This poem explores shyness and the desire to blend in.

chameleon kids are elusive
their skill is to rarely be found
drifting through days undetected
blending with those they're around

chameleon kids are careful
their secrets are never revealed
camouflage acting as armour
means feelings are safely concealed

some of them yearn to burn brightly
but predators lurk everywhere
so they learn to disguise any fire in their eyes
until not even they know it's there

Ball of Yarn

Shuntarō Tanikawa, translated by **William I. Elliott** and **Kazuo Kawamura**

This poem describes the journey of a ball of yarn.

Plump and snug and feathery,
a ball of yarn
rolls gaily down the street
and turns the corner.
No map,
no thermos bottle,
the knitting abandoned,
it's already crossed the bridge
and passed the police station,
and now
turns another corner.
Three years ago
it was all five fingers
of a lovely glove.

What a to-do!
Claudine Toutoungi

This poem describes the qualities of different animals.

The hammerhead's toothy. The kangaroo's pouchy.
The barn owl *to-wits* and sometimes *to-woohs*.

The lion is raspy. The crocodile's graspy.
The panda is dozy and chews on bamboo.

The wild boar is haughty. The tarantula's crawly.
The fox cub is crafty and learning kung fu.

The parrot is flouncy. The jaguar's pouncy.
The dormouse is sneezy and often *achoos*.

The clownfish is wobbly. The oyster is nobbly.
The jellyfish stings with a sting sharp and true.

They trumpet and splutter, flip, flop and flutter.
it's a jamboree jackpot tip-top to-do!

Song of the Witches
William Shakespeare

This poem depicts a bubbling cauldron and the potion within it.

Double, double toil and trouble:
Fire, burn; and, cauldron, bubble.

Fillet of a fenny snake,
In the cauldron boil and bake;
Eye of newt, and toe of frog,
Wool of bat, and tongue of dog,
Adder's fork, and blind-worm's sting,
Lizard's leg, and howlet's wing,
For a charm of powerful trouble,
Like a hell-broth boil and bubble.

Double, double toil and trouble:
Fire, burn; and, cauldron, bubble.

Level 1 Speaking Verse and Prose: Grade 1

Bush Fire

Jackie Kay

This poem personifies a wild, raging fire.

That fire, they said, was red as red as red
as red as a fox, your lips, a cherry;
that fire, they said spread and spread and spread,
faster than a cheetah or a nasty rumour;
that fire, they said, was hot, so hot, so hot,
hotter than lava or an African summer.

That fire, they said, was angry, very angry.
For three roaring days, it danced wildly, wildly, wildly.
Wild as flamenco, strip the willow, a Highland fling.
That fire, they said, had a big bad mouth,
swearing, spluttering, 'Bring it on! Bring it on!'

That fire, they said, wolfed down the lot –
the lovely little homes, the trees, the land.
That fire, they said, left nothing behind at all:
one blackened trail, one sad scorched story.

The Blue-Green Stream

Wang Wei, translated by **Amy Lowell**

This Speaker travels to a river where they find peace and tranquillity.

Every time I have started for the Yellow Flower River,
I have gone down the Blue-Green Stream,
Following the hills, making ten thousand turnings.
We go along rapidly, but advance scarcely one hundred *li*.
We are in the midst of a noise of water,
Of the confused and mingled sounds of water broken by stones,
And in the deep darkness of pine-trees.
Rocked, rocked,
Moving on and on,
We float past water-chestnuts
Into a still clearness reflecting reeds and rushes.
My heart is clean and white as silk; it has already achieved Peace;
It is smooth as the placid river.
I love to stay here, curled up on the rocks,
Dropping my fish-line forever.

Whenever you see a tree

Padma Venkatraman

This cleverly shaped poem describes the life cycle of a tree.

Think
how many long years
this tree waited as a seed
for an animal or bird or wind or rain
to maybe carry it to maybe the right spot
where again it waited months for seasons to change
until time and temperature were fine enough to coax it
to swell and burst its hard shell so it could send slender roots
to clutch at grains of soil and let tender shoots reach toward the sun
Think how many decades or centuries it thickened and climbed and grew
taller and deeper never knowing if it would find enough water or light
or when conditions would be right so it could keep on spreading leaves
adding blossoms and dancing
Next time
you see
a tree
think
how
much
hope
it holds

Say How You Feel
Joseph Coelho

This poem uses images of the natural world to describe different emotions.

When I'm sad
it feels like the sky is crashing down,
like the oceans are rising
and the ground is swallowing me up.
All is dark and cold.

When I'm nervous
it feels like my heart
is going to lightning-strike out of my chest,
like my skin is raining,
like my belly is a mudslide.

When I'm happy
my cheeks feel like rose buds,
my tummy glows with sunlight,
my shoulders are a forest breeze.

When I'm angry
my body is rock,
my face is wet clay.
Meteorites inhabit my fists,
my voice is all smoke and fire.

When I'm excited
my toes are ants,
I'm a river bubbling
and an air current of wishes,
my smile could explode the sun.

Riddle
Anna Laetitia Barbauld

This poem is a riddle, where the Speaker describes the qualities of a hidden subject.

From rosy bowers we issue forth,
From east to west, from south to north,
Unseen, unfelt, by night, by day,
Abroad we take our airy way:
We foster love and kindle strife,
The bitter and the sweet of life:
Piercing and sharp, we wound like steel;
Now, smooth as oil, those wounds we heal:
Not strings of pearl are valued more,
Or gems enchased in golden ore;
Yet thousands of us every day,
Worthless and vile, are thrown away.
Ye wise, secure with bars of brass
The double doors through which we pass;
For, once escaped, back to our cell
No human art can us compel.

Advice from a Caterpillar

Rachel Rooney

In this poem, a caterpillar gives advice to their younger self.

When I was egg, I too, clung onto leaf
in shaded safety, hidden underside.
And fastened by a pinprick of belief
I dared to dream I was a butterfly.

A hunger hatched. I ate the home I knew
then inched along the disappearing green.
In shedding every skin that I outgrew,
became a hundred times the size I'd been.

And now I'm spinning silk to fix my spot.
Outside remains. Inside I'm changing things.
This caterpillar's planning on the lot;
proboscis and antennae, four bright wings.

So keep on clinging on, my ovoid one.
For who you are has only just begun.

The Music of Beauty

James Nack

This poem communicates the power of visual beauty.

To me thy lips are mute, but when I gaze
Upon thee in thy perfect loveliness, –
No trait that should not be – no lineament
To jar with the exquisite harmony
Of Beauty's music, breathing to the eyes,
I pity those who think they pity me;
Who drink the tide that gushes from thy lips
Unconscious of its sweets, as if they were
E'en as I am – and turn their marble eyes
Upon thy loveliness, without the thrill
That maddens me with joy's delirium.

The Land of Nod
Robert Louis Stevenson

This Speaker describes the adventures of their dreams.

From breakfast on through all the day
At home among my friends I stay;
But every night I go abroad
Afar into the land of Nod.

All by myself I have to go,
With none to tell me what to do –
All alone beside the streams
And up the mountain-sides of dreams.

The strangest things are there for me,
Both things to eat and things to see,
And many frightening sights abroad
Till morning in the land of Nod.

Try as I like to find the way,
I never can get back by day,
Nor can remember plain and clear
The curious music that I hear.

Level 1 Speaking Verse and Prose: Grade 2 – Verse

Home

Rosa Terry (Runner-up in LAMDA Learners' Poetry Prize 2023)

This poem explores the meaning of home.

If home was a place,
I'd visit each and every day,
If home was a view
I'd take a picture and print it,
If home was a holiday,
I'd jump on the next flight,
If home was a flower
I'd place it in my hair,
If home was a perfume
I'd spritz myself from head to toe,
If home was the sea,
I'd dive in without fear,
If home was a tree,
I'd climb up to the highest branch.
Even if it were unsteady I'd know I was safe,
Even if the sea were choppy, I'd know I'd be ok,
Even if the flight was long, I wouldn't be bored.

If home was a house,
I wouldn't want to leave, would I?

But because home isn't these things,
Because home is you,
I'll hold you much tighter,
I'll hug you for longer,
And I'll remain by your side,
For together we are stronger.

December, 1919

Claude McKay

This poem explores grief and the Speaker's struggle to express their emotions.

Last night I heard your voice, mother,
The words you sang to me
When I, a little barefoot boy,
Knelt down against your knee.

And tears gushed from my heart, mother,
And passed beyond its wall,
But though the fountain reached my throat
The drops refused to fall.

'Tis ten years since you died, mother,
Just ten dark years of pain,
And oh, I only wish that I
Could weep just once again.

A Tip of the Slongue

Joseph Coelho

This Speaker uses spoonerisms to describe their day at school.

Today I had a tip of the slongue
  I mean a slip of the tongue.

    I told my teacher,
    'I'm so sorry, sir,
but my mords are all in a wuddle.'

'Stop being so billy, soy,' he said.
    'You've got me noing it dow!'
And the whole class lurst out baughing.

    'It's not my fault, sir,' I said.
      'I han't celp it!'

    And now the whole class
  are challing about their fairs
  and rolling on the loor flaughing.

    'That's enough,' said Sir.
'Any more and I'll send you to the Heputy Deadmaster.
    It's not smart or clever,
    you are not being a fart smeller!'

Superpowers

Ruth Awolola

This poem portrays the bond between two siblings.

My little brother loves superheroes.
He wants to change the world,
get the keys to the city and save the girl.

I watch the films with him all the time,
whenever he is sad,
whenever he really wants our mum and dad.

When we're late to school
and we're running down the street,
I tell him he's the fastest man that I'll ever meet.

And I can't deny he's strong,
with all he has to do,
though he's yet to master the art of Jujitsu.

Our parents must think we're clever,
they let us do everything on our own:
cook, clean and take care of the home.

I think we might have powers,
the ones that are most believable.
I think to our parents
we might be invisible.

This World is not Conclusion

Emily Dickinson

This poem considers attitudes towards life after death.

This World is not conclusion.
A Species stands beyond –
Invisible, as Music –
But positive, as Sound –
It beckons, and it baffles –
Philosophy, don't know –
And through a Riddle, at the last –
Sagacity, must go –
To guess it, puzzles scholars –
To gain it, Men have borne
Contempt of Generations
And Crucifixion, shown –
Faith slips – and laughs, and rallies –
Blushes, if any see –
Plucks at a twig of Evidence –
And asks a Vane, the way –
Much Gesture, from the Pulpit –
Strong Hallelujahs roll –
Narcotics cannot still the Tooth
That nibbles at the soul –

Filter
Suma Subramaniam

This poem celebrates heritage, community and culture.

I come from a country so far away
that you may have visited only in your dreams.
My face does not bear the pale color of my palms.
I don't speak your language at home.
I don't even sound like you.
If you come to my house, you'll see my family:
my mother in a sari,
my father wearing a sacred thread around his body,
and me, eating a plate of spicy biryani
instead of a burger or pizza
at the dinner table.
If you, for a moment, shed your filter,
you will also see my pockets filled with Tootsie Rolls,
waiting to be shared with you.

From On the Beach at Night
Walt Whitman

This poem depicts the power and vastness of the universe.

On the beach at night,
Stands a child with her father,
Watching the east, the autumn sky.

Up through the darkness,
While ravening clouds, the burial clouds, in black masses spreading,
Lower sullen and fast athwart and down the sky,
Amid a transparent clear belt of ether yet left in the east,
Ascends large and calm the lord-star Jupiter,
And nigh at hand, only a very little above,
Swim the delicate sisters the Pleiades.

From the beach the child holding the hand of her father,
Those burial-clouds that lower victorious soon to devour all,
Watching, silently weeps.

Extinct

Monika Johnson

This futuristic poem explores a world where humans have been replaced by robots.

The year is 3036
and robots rule the world.
Half animal, half mad machine
they clunk,
and growl,
and whirr.

The humans died off long ago
extinct for 90 years.
Devoured by computers.
Disconnected.
Disappeared.

Their brains just couldn't hack it
their cells devoid of matter.
Chomped up by screens
and mad machines,
no space for thoughts or Chatter.

A new world awaits us –
one of robots, tech and wires.
No need for food or exercise
and never to expire.

And if that thought alarms you –
no contact, talk or hugs,
there's no need to panic –
we'll disconnect you at the plug.

Level 1 Speaking Verse and Prose: Grade 2 – Prose

Contact

Malorie Blackman

This novel is set in the future where touch is forbidden, and everyone must wear non-contact (NC) suits. But Cal and his friends are tired of playing by the rules. They want to feel alive. In this section, they organise a real-life game of football.

'Is it safe to play?' Andrew asked.

'Course it is,' Cal said, and he began to take off his NC suit.

The others looked around before they did the same.

They always waited for Cal to take off his NC suit first. He and Andrew had been the first ones to play football without their suits. Then Tariq and Jenna had joined in – and then, over many months, their numbers had grown to ten true and trusted friends.

Cal kicked off his NC suit and stood in his shorts, NC boots and a T-shirt. The others did the same. Cal took a deep breath and raised his hands to the sky. The air dancing over his skin felt like a whisper from heaven. A slight breeze blew. It was amazing to think that, a year ago, Cal hadn't even known how good a breeze could feel as it sighed across his face.

Cal and the others stood in a circle, hand in hand. Cal marvelled at the feel of real fingers. Not virtual fingers or fingers enclosed in an NC glove but real live fingers! Clammy, sweaty, warm, soft, wonderful fingers! Even the best NC suit couldn't match that feeling of contact.

'Ready?' Cal asked everyone.

They all nodded.

'All for one and one for all and no one must know!' they all chanted. 'Let's play!'

Tariq threw out the ball – it was a home-made one they'd made out of scrap plastic packed with soft wadding – and the game began.

Real tackles. Contact!

Real elbows. Contact!

And then Andrew scored a goal. Everyone gathered round him to pat him on the back or hug him or lift him into the air, even the players on the other side.

Cal beamed at everyone as they ran up and down the pitch. It was like being truly human for one afternoon a month. Only on this wasteland pitch did he feel alive. He loved its rough, broken surface – nothing like the perfect green grass of the virtual pitch. The result didn't matter. The game did. No screens, no computer programs, just real kids! Cal felt sure that flying and swooping and soaring couldn't be any better than the contact of real football.

Chapter 5, 'Kit' – Chapter 6, 'Pitch'

There May Be a Castle

Piers Torday

Following a car crash, Mouse wakes up in a magical landscape and embarks on an extraordinary adventure. Mouse's quest leads him and his friends – including Nonky – towards finding a castle. This section explores Nonky's reaction to seeing the castle.

Nonky didn't join in. She watched them all shouting and jigging, but there was no trace of a smile on her face. Slowly she turned about and clopped into the shade of a large oak tree, from where she stood and watched them. Her tail drooped, and her eyes softened as she watched the others play sword-fighting with Dragnet.

'What is it, Nonky?' Mouse ran to the horse's side. 'Come and play. We've found the castle! Just like you asked!'

'Yes, thank you,' muttered the horse. 'I may only have one eye but I'm not blind.'

'So why are you being so boring?'

With a sigh, the great horse turned her head away from him. Mouse could not read her expression. But he noticed the single tear that welled up from deep inside her, rolling down her nose and on to the soft ground below.

He didn't understand.

Nonky was rude and mean. Nonky made sarcastic jokes and scoffed at everything. Nonky kept him going, even when he wanted to sit down in the middle of the track and cry. Yet now they had found what she had been nagging him to find all along, she didn't seem pleased or happy.

He looked up at her again, and in the horse's golden eyepatch he caught a glimpse of a child's face, reflected back at him as if from a shimmering pond.

And he realised.

'It's the castle. It's made you sad, hasn't it? Why did you want me to find it so badly if it was only going to make you cry?'

At first the horse couldn't reply, as if something was stuck in her throat. Mouse hugged her close, brushing off the clods of muddy snow.

'Finally,' said Nonky, her voice sounding cracked and strange. 'The first intelligent question you've asked'.

Chapter 28

Sad Book

Michael Rosen

Sometimes, Michael feels sad. It's mainly when he thinks about his son Eddie, who died. In this section, Michael describes what his sadness is like.

Sometimes this makes me really angry. I say to myself, 'How dare he go and die like that? How dare he make me sad.' He doesn't say anything, because he's not there anymore.

Sometimes I want to talk about all this to someone. Like my mum. But she's not here any more either. So I can't. I find someone else. And I tell them all about it.

Sometimes I don't want to talk about it. Not to anyone. No one. No one at all. I just want to think about it on my own. Because it's mine. And no one else's.

Sometimes because I'm sad I do crazy things – like shouting in the shower… banging a spoon on the table… or making my cheeks go whooph, boooph, whooph. Sometimes because I'm sad I do bad things. I can't tell you what they are. They are too bad. And it's not fair on the cat.

Sometimes I'm sad and I don't know why. It's just a cloud that comes along and covers me up. It's not because Eddie's gone. It's not because my mum's gone. It's just because. Maybe it's because things now aren't like they were a few years ago. Like my family. It's not the same as it was a few years ago. So what happens is that there's a sad place inside me because things aren't the same.

I've been trying to figure out ways of being sad that don't hurt so much. Here are some of them: I tell myself that everyone has sad stuff. I'm not the only one. Maybe you have some too. Every day I try to do one thing I can be proud of. Then, when I go to bed, I think very, very, very hard about this one thing. I tell myself that being sad isn't the same as being horrible. I'm sad, not bad. Every day I try to do one thing that means I have a good time. It can be anything so long as it doesn't make anyone else unhappy.

Anne of Green Gables
Lucy Maud Montgomery

Anne is an eleven-year-old orphan who has been sent to live at Green Gables. She becomes best friends with Diana Barry. To celebrate Diana's birthday, the girls plan to attend a Debating Club concert. This section portrays Anne's excitement towards the event.

For Anne the real excitement began with the dismissal of school and increased therefrom in crescendo until it reached to a crash of positive ecstasy in the concert itself. They had a 'perfectly elegant tea;' and then came the delicious occupation of dressing in Diana's little room upstairs. Diana did Anne's front hair in the new pompadour style and Anne tied Diana's bows with the especial knack she possessed; and they experimented with at least half a dozen different ways of arranging their back hair. At last they were ready, cheeks scarlet and eyes glowing with excitement.

True, Anne could not help a little pang when she contrasted her plain black tam and shapeless, tight-sleeved, homemade gray-cloth coat with Diana's jaunty fur cap and smart little jacket. But she remembered in time that she had an imagination and could use it.

Then Diana's cousins, the Murrays from Newbridge, came; they all crowded into the big pung sleigh, among straw and furry robes. Anne reveled in the drive to the hall, slipping along over the satin-smooth roads with the snow crisping under the runners. There was a magnificent sunset, and the snowy hills and deep-blue water of the St. Lawrence Gulf seemed to rim in the splendor like a huge bowl of pearl and sapphire brimmed with wine and fire. Tinkles of sleigh bells and distant laughter, that seemed like the mirth of wood elves, came from every quarter.

'Oh, Diana,' breathed Anne, squeezing Diana's mittened hand under the fur robe, 'isn't it all like a beautiful dream? Do I really look the same as usual? I feel so different that it seems to me it must show in my looks.'

'You look awfully nice,' said Diana, who having just received a compliment from one of her cousins, felt that she ought to pass it on. 'You've got the loveliest color.'

Chapter 19, 'A Concert a Catastrophe and a Confession'

The Chronicles of Narnia: The Magician's Nephew
C. S. Lewis

Digory Kirke and Polly Plummer are friends. Prior to this section, Digory's mysterious Uncle Andrew tricks Polly into wearing a yellow ring, which causes her to vanish to another world. Uncle Andrew explains to Digory that while yellow rings can transport someone to another world, green rings can transport someone back. Therefore, Digory follows Polly to the other world, and in this section, they experiment with their rings.

'Blast and botheration!' exclaimed Digory. 'What's gone wrong now? We've put our yellow rings on all right. He said yellow for the outward journey.'

Now the truth was that Uncle Andrew, who knew nothing about the Wood between the Worlds, had quite a wrong idea about the rings. The yellow ones weren't 'outward' rings and the green ones weren't 'homeward' rings; at least, not in the way he thought. The stuff of which both were made had all come from the wood. The stuff in the yellow rings had the power of drawing you into the wood; it was stuff that wanted to get back to its own place, the in-between place. But the stuff in the green rings is stuff that is trying to get out of its place; so that a green ring would take you out of the wood and into a world. Uncle Andrew, you see, was working with things he did not really understand; most magicians are. Of course Digory did not realize the truth quite clearly either, or not till later. But when they talked it over, they decided to try their green rings on the new pool, just to see what happened.

'I'm game if you are,' said Polly. But she really said this because, in her heart of hearts, she now felt sure that neither kind of ring was going to work at all in the new pool, and so there was nothing worse to be afraid of than another splash. I am not quite sure that Digory had not the same feeling. At any rate, when they had both put on their greens and come back to the edge of the water, and taken hands again, they were certainly a good deal more cheerful and less solemn than they had been in the first time.

'One – Two – Three – Go!' said Digory. And they jumped.

Chapter 3, 'The Wood Between the Worlds'

Sona Sharma, Looking After Planet Earth

Chitra Soundar

Sona has been learning about climate change in school and cares deeply about Planet Earth. To save electricity, Sona turns all the lights off during a school concert. In this section, Sona stands on stage and tells the audience her reasons for doing so.

Onstage, Sona stood on tiptoes to speak into the microphone. She leaned in and knocked on the mic. SCREECH! The hall quietened.

'I'm sorry I turned off the mic and lights,' she said.

'Good girl,' said Miss Rao, trying to nudge her away from the mic.

But Sona wouldn't budge. She had to tell everyone it wasn't a prank. She was just trying to look after the planet.

'My friends and I are very worried about Planet Earth,' she said into the mic. 'What if the planet gets too hot by the time we grow up? What if the oceans are so dirty that we can never go to the beach? We must all do something to protect our planet – switch off lights and speakers, find alternatives to plastic. It just piles up in landfill and never dies.'

Sona couldn't go on. She wiped her nose and face on her sleeve and tried not to cry. Her legs were still trembling.

Miss Rao came to her rescue. 'Sona's class has been working on a project about looking after the planet,' she said. 'They've been discovering that we can all help. Every little action goes a long way – like turning off lights when we don't need them or walking to the auditorium instead of driving if we live close by. Start small, start now,' said Miss Rao.

'Do more, do it now,' said Sona into the mic. Then she ran off the stage to the green room.

But inside the green room, the President sat like a simmering pot of sambhar full of chillies.

'What a drama, Sona! You should be ashamed of yourself,' she said.

'Sona is looking after our planet. And she has bravely apologized to an entire hall full of strangers. There is nothing to be ashamed of.'

Sona smiled. Amma was on her side.

Chapter 4, 'Super Proud'

The Selfish Giant
Oscar Wilde

The Selfish Giant does not like children playing in his garden. To stop them, he puts up a sign which reads: 'Trespassers Will Be Prosecuted'. This section explores the consequences of the Selfish Giant's actions.

The poor children had now nowhere to play. They tried to play on the road, but the road was very dusty and full of hard stones, and they did not like it. They used to wander round the high wall when their lessons were over, and talk about the beautiful garden inside. 'How happy we were there,' they said to each other.

Then the Spring came, and all over the country there were little blossoms and little birds. Only in the garden of the Selfish Giant it was still winter. The birds did not care to sing in it as there were no children, and the trees forgot to blossom. Once a beautiful flower put its head out from the grass, but when it saw the notice-board it was so sorry for the children that it slipped back into the ground again, and went off to sleep. The only people who were pleased were the Snow and the Frost. 'Spring has forgotten this garden,' they cried, 'so we will live here all the year round.' The Snow covered up the grass with her great white cloak, and the Frost painted all the trees silver. Then they invited the North Wind to stay with them, and he came. He was wrapped in furs, and he roared all day about the garden, and blew the chimney-pots down. 'This is a delightful spot,' he said, 'we must ask the Hail on a visit.' So the Hail came. Every day for three hours he rattled on the roof of the castle till he broke most of the slates, and then he ran round and round the garden as fast as he could go. He was dressed in grey, and his breath was like ice.

'I cannot understand why the Spring is so late in coming,' said the Selfish Giant, as he sat at the window and looked out at his cold white garden; 'I hope there will be a change in the weather.'

But the Spring never came, nor the Summer. The Autumn gave golden fruit to every garden, but to the Giant's garden she gave none.

A Different Kind of Princess Story

Aimee McGoldrick

Cassandra is a princess who does not want to follow her family's rules. In this section, she reflects on her upbringing and education, whilst dreaming of a different future for herself.

I never went to school. I was taught at home. I had no friends. None. I never left the castle grounds unless it was a Royal visit to another country, where I'd sit in another castle, not that different to my own and smile. Otherwise, I would literally sit in my room or wander the castle grounds by myself. I mean I would talk to the gardener or the maids but, that wasn't the same. Not what I needed. I craved someone my own age. I was desperate to be in a classroom with school friends. Honestly, if you are reading this and you go to school, don't ever complain. Living without it was horrible. I mean don't get me wrong I learnt lots from my tutors. I had the best teachers in the world flown in to teach me. But, playtime by yourself, lunchtime by yourself, after school clubs BY YOURSELF is miserable. I didn't even have Freddie for those things. He would spend those with Daddy taking notes, learning how to be King. He is the next in line you see. The heir to the throne; which basically means that he will run The Tropics one day. I won't. So, why do I need to be locked in the tower I hear you ask? Good question. A very good question. One I would often ask my Father and he would reply:

'Cassandra (that's me - sorry, I haven't even introduced myself, silly me!) the world is a dangerous place. It is okay for Freddie, he will become King. He needs to know and understand the country. You on the other hand need to stop worrying about going out into the Kingdom and start thinking about finding a Prince; one who will look after you when I am gone, pay for you to have your own castle, pay for your jewels and look after you. You can't just marry a normal boy. You are a Princess!'

I did not want to marry. Not then and maybe not ever. I don't need a husband.

Level 1 Speaking Verse and Prose: Grade 3 – Verse

Can I Sit There?

Avni Patel (Winner of LAMDA Learners' Poetry Prize 2023)

This Speaker navigates friendships at school.

I entered through the school gates,
Feeling absolutely great!
Skipping down the school halls,
I ran when I heard the bell call.

In front of my desk was Clara Hamm,
I remember her from an Instagram!
She's definitely NOT the friend for me.
There's a girl beside her, who is she?

With a face full of blush, it's Olivia Cooke,
Her make-up hacks keep popping up on Facebook.
I'll have to look somewhere else,
This is getting really intense.

Oh, there's the cool smart boy, he claims,
His Snap story was really lame.
No surprise, he's got a dog,
Cheesy pictures all over his blog.

At the front of the class is the Tiktok queen,
She's only 11 but pretending she's a teen.
I'll never find a friend to be a part of my pack,
Hold fire, there's one more person, who's that at the back?

Incognito, it's Amelia Leed,
She's really shy and she likes to read.
Before class started, I ran up to an empty chair.
I smiled and asked Amelia, 'Can I sit there?'

Count That Day Lost
George Eliot (Mary Ann Evans)

This poem explores everyday acts of kindness.

If you sit down at the set of sun
And count the acts that you have done,
And, counting, find
One self-denying deed, one word
That eased the heart of him who heard,
One glance most kind
That fell like sunshine where it went –
Then you may count that day well spent.

But if, through all the livelong day,
You've cheered no heart, by yea or nay –
If, through it all
You've nothing done that you can trace
That brought the sunshine to one face –
No act most small
That helped some soul and nothing cost –
Then count that day as worse than lost.

Difficult Damsels

Nikita Gill

This poem celebrates women who are fierce, brave and powerful.

Not all girls are made of sugar
and spice and all things nice.

These are girls made of dark lace
and witchcraft and a little bit of vice.

These are daughters made claw first
and story-mad, tiger roar and wolf-bad.

These are women made of terrible tempests
and savage storms and the untamed unwanted.

These are damsels made of flawless fearlessness
made of more bravery than knights have ever seen.

These are princesses made of valour and poison alike
and they are here to hold court as your queens.

Comparative Guidance for Social Distancing

Brian Bilston

This poem describes the two-metre social distancing rule, implemented during the pandemic.

Just remember it's:
The length of a musk ox or fully-grown llama
Three Rubik's Cubes plus one Keir Starmer
Eleven seven-inch singles by Bananarama
That's what two metres is.
Alternatively, it's:
1/192,199,930th of a single moon beam
2.2 times greater than Munch's The Scream
About 10½ packets of custard creams
That'll be two metres.
If easier, think:
Thirty-three pairs of dragonfly wings
The length of a yoga mat belonging to Sting
Two one-metre long pieces of string
That comes to two metres.
Or failing that, imagine:
0.00000091 of the coast of mainland Wales
18.2648402 cricket bails
One and a quarter Prunella Scales
That's two metres.

We Wear the Mask

Paul Laurence Dunbar

This poem explores oppression in a prejudiced society.

We wear the mask that grins and lies,
It hides our cheeks and shades our eyes, –
This debt we pay to human guile;
With torn and bleeding hearts we smile,
And mouth with myriad subtleties.

Why should the world be over-wise,
In counting all our tears and sighs?
Nay, let them only see us, while
    We wear the mask.

We smile, but, oh great Christ, our cries
To thee from tortured souls arise.
We sing, but oh the clay is vile
Beneath our feet, and long the mile,
But let the world dream otherwise,
    We wear the mask!

I skipped school today

Kwame Alexander

This poem explores declining mental health.

and drank soda
and didn't eat lunch
and I almost got arrested
and I hate math
and tomorrow we have to play basketball in gym class
and I'm not that good
and I'm not that good at anything
and who's gonna teach me everything?
and do I need to get a job?
and why is everybody always sorry?
and CJ's dad is soooo cool
and I'm not taking a shower tonight
because I didn't do anything all day
but read comics
and play Pac-Man
and I still don't feel
any better
than I did
last week
or yesterday
or when I woke up
and I'm tired
so can I please
just stay
in my room
turn out the lights
and hide
inside the darkness
that owns me?
Please.

Charlie, I asked you how was school?

Something About That Day

Kirsten Charters

This poem contemplates responses to change.

There was something about that day,
The way the wind howled,
But the clouds stood still.
I felt something in my bones,
Though I couldn't be sure,
Some change is afoot,
Something new,
Something old,
I liked it, I didn't,
I do and I don't.

I welcomed this day with open arms,
although I was tempted to shy away.
New beginnings, closed doors.
Open your heart to a world that's new,
It's scary, it's nothing, it's totally you.

The sun breaks through the thick cloud,
A symbol of hope and a new found peace.
I'm with you in spirit, I heard someone say,
It stayed with me that did, for the rest of the day.

There was something in the air that day,
There was something about that day.

I Shall Return

Claude McKay

This poem portrays a longing for home.

I shall return again; I shall return
To laugh and love and watch with wonder-eyes
At golden noon the forest fires burn,
Wafting their blue-black smoke to sapphire skies.
I shall return to loiter by the streams
That bathe the brown blades of the bending grasses,
And realize once more my thousand dreams
Of waters rushing down the mountain passes.
I shall return to hear the fiddle and fife
Of village dances, dear delicious tunes
That stir the hidden depths of native life,
Stray melodies of dim remembered runes.
I shall return, I shall return again,
To ease my mind of long, long years of pain.

Level 1 Speaking Verse and Prose: Grade 3 – Prose

Ghost

Jason Reynolds

Ghost is a runner. He has been running for all the wrong reasons, until he meets Coach, who helps him build technique, stamina and power. In this section, it is race day. Ghost is at the starting line where he is taunted by his competitor Brandon Simmons. Ghost's friend Lu helps him get his head back in the game before the race begins.

Lu pulled me into him, grabbed me by the back of my neck. 'It's me and you,' he said, snapping me out of my Brandon Simmons nightmare state and back into focus. Had I known Brandon was a runner, I would've told Dre and Red to come to the meet just so they could see me smoke him. Shoot, I might've invited the whole school. Even Principal Marshall. Maybe even would've told Shamika to bring that laugh with her for this special occasion. Lu gave me five, then repeated 'It's me' – he pointed to himself – 'and you.' He put his finger on my chest.

I was in lane six, Lu in lane one. I bent down, untied my silver shoes, then retied them. I looked around at the crowd, a smear of people rooting for their friend or son or brother or teammate. Somebody was probably there even rooting for Brandon. Then I looked over at the side where the Defenders were, Coach clapping, a proud grin on his face. Sunny cheering, an orange slice in his mouth, the peel like a bright mouthpiece. And Patty – who by the way had on shiny lip stuff and had her hair greased and slicked straight back – squatted down and stared, almost like she was mind-beaming speed into me. She nodded. I nodded. My mother, looking at me with wet eyes. She waved. And all I could think about at that moment was the two of us running down the hall three years ago.

'On your mark!' said the starter. My heart *thump-thumped*, *thump-thumped*, and I could feel my insides turning colours. I'm not sure what colour. Not red. Not blue. Something else. Something different. A colour I never felt before. I squatted down, pushed my feet back against the blocks, stretched out my thumbs and index fingers and placed them on the edge of the white starting line. Rested my weight on my arms. Closed my eyes. Thought of us running to the door. Running for our lives.

'Get set!' said the starter. Butts in the air. The sound of the gun cocking. The sound of the door unlocking. Heart pounding. Breathe. Breathe. Breathe. Silence.

This. Is. It.

And then... BOOM!

Chapter 10, 'Race Day'

Waiting for Anya

Michael Morpurgo

Set in France during World War Two, a young shepherd named Jo befriends a German Corporal. In this section, the Corporal reflects on why German troops are patrolling the village.

It was several minutes before Jo found the courage to be able to speak of it but he knew he had to. 'About what happened to your daughter,' he said. 'I'm sorry, everyone's sorry.'

'Thank you, Jo,' said the Corporal. 'Thank you.' And then he started talking and once he had started he didn't stop. 'If there has to be a war', he said, 'then it should be fought between soldiers. Before, it was always between soldiers, that I can understand. I do not like it, but I can understand it. At Verdun it was one soldier in a uniform against another soldier in another uniform. What have women and children to do with fighting wars, tell me that? Every day since I hear about my daughter, every day I ask myself many questions and I try to answer them. It is not so easy. What are we doing here, Wilhelm, I ask myself? Answer: I'm guarding the frontier. Question: why? Answer: to stop people escaping. Question: why do they want to escape? Answer: because they are in fear of their lives. Question: who are these people? Answer: Frenchmen who do not want to be taken to work in Germany, maybe a few prisoners-of-war escaping, and Jews. Question: who is it that threatens the lives of Jews? Answer: we do. Question: why? Answer: there is no answer. Question: and when they are captured, what happens? Answer: concentration camp. Question: and then? Answer: no answer, not because there is no answer, Jo, but because we are frightened to know the answer.' He wiped his cheeks with the back of his hand and laughed. 'You see what happens when you ask so many questions, Jo? When I was little I always asked too many questions and my mother would become impatient. When I asked why again and again she would say, 'a blue reason, Willi, a blue reason'.' Jo smiled at that. 'So,' said the Corporal, 'we smile again. We must smile. It is good to smile. Now we look for eagles.'

As they climbed out of the trees they left the mist below them and reached a wide plain of spongy grass, dotted with grey-blue thistles and scattered rocks, with a silver stream running through it.

Chapter 6

When Life Gives You Mangoes
Kereen Getten

Clara and Gaynah are supposed to be best friends, but recently Gaynah has not been acting like one. Frustrated and upset, Clara throws their shared memory box in the river, much to the anger of Gaynah's parents. In this section, Clara exposes Gaynah's secrets.

I find the memory box in my parents' room. On the chest of drawers. Next to a photo of Nana and me sitting under the mango tree. The blue top is gone, and so are the mirror and the pin. But the diary is still there.

I hover over the box.

Count, Clara, count.

I place my hands firmly on my hips and stare hard at Nana's photo, willing it to calm me down. I close my eyes.

One, two, three, four.

Maybe Mama kept the box hoping I would change my mind and want it back. She's wrong. I don't want it back, but I'm glad she kept it.

One, two, three, four, five.

I breathe heavily through my nose, my chest rising and falling.

Four, five, six, seven.

I don't want to be mad, but all I can see is Juliette's sneer and all I can hear is her evil voice taunting me. Then Pastor Brown's growly voice telling Mama and Papa I need to be punished. I grab the diary and return to the veranda as Papa tries calming everyone down.

I flick the diary open under the glare of the veranda light, my chest pumping fast. I don't need to read the pages. I know every page by heart.

'Gaynah Campbell cheated on the maths test when she was nine because she didn't know her eight times table. Gaynah doesn't like it when you make her corned beef sandwiches; she gives them to the dog outside school and tells you a bully from the high school stole them, but she can never remember his name because HE DOESN'T EXIST. Gaynah has a crush on Calvin Brown and that's the only reason she begged you to let her have private Bible study at Pastor Brown's house. Gaynah Campbell wishes her mother didn't teach at our school because she is embarrassed by the old granny clothes she wears.' I catch my breath.

Everyone is staring at me in horror. Juliette's mouth twists from side to side like a snake slithering towards you before it opens its jaw to swallow you whole.

Mama has that look again. The one of desperation.

'Clara' is all she manages.

Chapter 7

West African Folk-Tales

W. H. Barker and **Cecilia Sinclair**

When Anansi's hometown experiences famine, Anansi is determined to find his family some food. He spies a tiny island in the middle of the sea. Believing there to be food upon this island, Anansi makes the journey across the water, but is dismayed to return empty handed. Upon leaving the island, he throws himself into the water. Miraculously, he finds himself at the bottom of the sea, where he is gifted a food-producing pot.

Being anxious to test the pot at once, Anansi only waited till he was again seated in the old boat to say, 'Pot, pot, what you used to do for your master do now for me.' Immediately good food of all sorts appeared. Anansi ate a hearty meal, which he very much enjoyed.

On reaching land again, his first thought was to run home and give all his family a good meal from his wonderful pot. A selfish, greedy fear prevented him. 'What if I should use up all the magic of the pot on them, and have nothing more left for myself! Better keep the pot a secret – then I can enjoy a meal when I want one.' So, his mind full of this thought, he hid the pot.

He reached home, pretending to be utterly worn out with fatigue and hunger. There was not a grain of food to be had anywhere. His wife and poor children were weak with want of it, but selfish Anansi took no notice of that. He congratulated himself at the thought of his magic pot, now safely hidden in his room. There he retired from time to time when he felt hungry, and enjoyed a good meal. His family got thinner and thinner, but he grew plumper and plumper. They began to suspect some secret, and determined to find it out. His eldest son, Kweku Tsin, had the power of changing himself into any shape he chose; so he took the form of a tiny fly, and accompanied his father everywhere. At last, Anansi, feeling hungry, entered his room and closed the door. Next he took the pot, and had a fine meal. Having replaced the pot in its hiding-place, he went out, on the pretence of looking for food.

As soon as he was safely out of sight, Kweku Tsin fetched out the pot and called all his hungry family to come at once. They had as good a meal as their father had had. When they had finished, Mrs Anansi – to punish her husband – said she would take the pot down to the village and give everybody a meal.

Part 1, 'Anansi, Or Spider, Tales'; Chapter 4, 'Thunder and Anansi'

The Traitor Game

B. R. Collins

Michael and Francis are the inventors of a secret fantasy world called Evgard. When their imaginative world is discovered, Michael immediately blames Francis and gets revenge by exposing Francis' secrets to the school bully Shipley. In this section, Michael and Shipley are arguing, and Shipley pushes Michael out of a first-floor window.

He didn't remember landing.

But he did. He must have done.

'I'm fine. Really. I'm fine. I'm fine.' He kept saying it, over and over again, because no one seemed to believe him. After a while he started to think, *Maybe I should just shut up and let them work it out for themselves,* but somehow he couldn't stop himself. He tried to stand up. 'Look. I'm fine. Watch. I'm perfectly *fine –*' but someone laid a restraining hand on his arm and pushed him firmly back into the smashed flower bed.

'Just stay still, Michael. You're going to be all right.'

'I *know*, that's what I said, I'm absolutely –' but Father Markham wasn't listening. Michael raised one arm and waved it around. '*Look*. Everything's fine. I'm fine. I'm really –' A drop of blood rolled back down his wrist and soaked into his shirt-cuff. He thought, *Oops. Mum'll go ballistic if I've torn this shirt.*

'All right, Michael. I heard you. Calm down. We're just waiting for the ambulance.'

'I don't need an ambulance. I'm fine...' but no one took any notice. Michael dropped his head back and stared up into the rain. A crowd had gathered; someone was trying to shoo them away. He thought, *This is stupid. I'm perfectly all right.*

He heard the paramedics before he saw them; conferring with Father Markham in low voices, 'Fell out of a window? That one there, on the first floor?' and Father Markham saying, 'The one that's broken, yes...'

But even the paramedics didn't take any notice of him. When they leant over he tried to tell them he was fine, really, he was fine, and they swapped a look that

said, *Hmm, looks like this one's in shock, he can't stop talking...* He said, 'Look, I'm *fine*, I don't need an ambulance, I'm fine, I'm just a bit –'

'Ok, mate, let's just take you to hospital, get you checked over.' It wasn't like he had a choice. In the end he just gave up and thought, *Stuff it, if they want to waste their time...*

Chapter 14

Heidi

Johanna Spyri, translated by **Louise Brooks**

Heidi is a young orphan girl who has gone to live with her grandfather, a goatherd, in the Swiss Alps. Heidi is in awe of her new home in the mountains. In this section, Heidi meets her grandfather's goats.

At last it was evening. The wind began to sigh through the old trees; as it blew harder, all the branches swayed back and forth. Heidi felt the sounds not only in her ears, but in her heart; and she was so happy, so happy, she ran out under the pines, and sprang and leaped for joy, as if she had found the greatest pleasure imaginable.

Her grandfather meanwhile stood in the doorway, and watched the child.

Suddenly a shrill whistle was heard. Heidi stopped her jumping, and the old man went out. Down from the mountain streamed the goats, one after the other, and Peter was in their midst.

With a joyous shout Heidi vanished into the midst of the flock, to greet her old friends of the morning, one and all.

When they reached the hut, they all stopped; and from out the herd came two beautiful slender goats, one white and one brown. They went to the old man, and licked his hands; for he held a little salt for them every evening when they came home. Peter vanished with the rest. Heidi stroked the goats gently, one after the other, then ran to the other side, and did the same. She was as joyful as possible over the charming creatures.

'Are they both ours, grandfather? Will they go into our stall? Will they always stay here with us?' Heidi poured out her questions in her excitement, her grandfather having hardly a chance to repeat a continual 'Yes, yes child,' now and then. When the goats had licked up all the salt, her grandfather said, 'Go fetch your little mug and some bread.'

Heidi obeyed; and he milked the goats into the mug, into which he cut bits of bread, and said: 'Now eat your supper, and then go to bed. Dete left another bundle for you, there are your night-gowns, and so on, in it. You will find them in the press. I must put up the goats now. Go, and sleep soundly.'

'Good-night, grandfather, good-night,' shouted Heidi after him, as he disappeared with the goats. 'What are their names?'

'The white one is called Schwänli, the other Bärli.'

'Good-night, Schwänli; good-night, Bärli,' shouted the child, at the top of her voice, to the goats, who were already going into their stall.

Chapter 2, 'At the Grandfather's'

A Kind of Spark

Elle McNicoll

Addie is campaigning for a memorial in memory of the witch trials that took place centuries ago in her Scottish hometown. In this section, Addie speaks to the village about her connection to the witches, and what they can do to remember them.

'Centuries ago, someone like me could have been accused of being a witch. Just for being different. I sometimes don't know how to read people or work out how they are feeling. This can lead to misunderstandings. Sometimes my face doesn't show how happy I really am. I might not seem that approachable. And I'm very easy to bully. Sometimes I even start to believe what the bullies are saying.'

I look at my hand. At Maggie's name.

'My sister Keedie is autistic, too. And she made friends with another autistic girl at her appointments. Her name was Bonnie. But, after Bonnie moved away, she couldn't cope anymore. With school, with her anxiety. So she got put away. By people who didn't understand her needs. No matter how much she tells them she needs to leave, they won't let her. They don't trust her, they don't think she knows herself.'

I sniff, feeling troubled as I remember Bonnie. The bright, laughing girl who had bad meltdowns but was never bad.

'If someone told me that I was a witch for long enough, I might have started to believe them. It seems easier sometimes, doesn't it? To believe the bad things instead of the good.'

I lose my place for a moment and look out at the faces. I don't know if it's me, but they seem to be really listening.

'When I heard what was done to these women, right here in Juniper, it hurt my heart. That they were killed merely for being different or weird, and everyone just let it happen and forgot.'

I see Mr Macintosh look down at his feet out of the corner of my eye.

'I don't want to forget them. I want us to have a plaque, something small, dedicated to their memory. Our apology.'

This was supposed to be the end of the speech but I decide to say one last thing.

'I think different is good. As long as you're not hurting anyone. We need all kinds of difference in the world. And I know some people think that I've been put up to this. All I can say is, if you believe that, you probably don't know any autistic girls.'

People laugh.

Chapter 20

The Wonderful Wizard of Oz

L. Frank Baum

Dorothy is in a magical but mysterious land, very far away from her home in Kansas. She must find the Wizard of Oz to help her get home. Along the way, she makes three friends: the Tin Man, the Scarecrow and the Cowardly Lion. In this section, they stumble across the lands of the Wicked Witch of the West, who attacks them with crows and bees.

The wild crows flew in one great flock toward Dorothy and her companions. When the little girl saw them coming she was afraid.

But the Scarecrow said, 'This is my battle, so lie down beside me and you will not be harmed.'

So they all lay upon the ground except the Scarecrow, and he stood up and stretched out his arms. And when the crows saw him they were frightened, as these birds always are by scarecrows, and did not dare to come any nearer. But the King Crow said:

'It is only a stuffed man. I will peck his eyes out.'

The King Crow flew at the Scarecrow, who caught it by the head and twisted its neck until it died. And then another crow flew at him, and the Scarecrow twisted its neck also. There were forty crows, and forty times the Scarecrow twisted a neck, until at last all were lying dead beside him. Then he called to his companions to rise, and again they went upon their journey.

When the Wicked Witch looked out again and saw all her crows lying in a heap, she got into a terrible rage, and blew three times upon her silver whistle.

Forthwith there was heard a great buzzing in the air, and a swarm of black bees came flying toward her.

'Go to the strangers and sting them to death!' commanded the Witch, and the bees turned and flew rapidly until they came to where Dorothy and her friends were walking. But the Woodman had seen them coming, and the Scarecrow had decided what to do.

'Take out my straw and scatter it over the little girl and the dog and the Lion,' he said to the Woodman, 'and the bees cannot sting them.' This the Woodman did,

and as Dorothy lay close beside the Lion and held Toto in her arms, the straw covered them entirely.

The bees came and found no one but the Woodman to sting, so they flew at him and broke off all their stings against the tin, without hurting the Woodman at all. And as bees cannot live when their stings are broken that was the end of the black bees, and they lay scattered thick about the Woodman, like little heaps of fine coal.

Chapter 12, 'The Search for the Wicked Witch'

Level 2 Speaking Verse and Prose: Grade 4 – Verse

Alexa, What is There to Know about Love?

Brian Bilston

This poem addresses questions to an Alexa on the topics of love, death and loneliness.

Alexa, what is there to know about love?
What is there to know about love?

A glove is a garment that covers the hand
for protection from the cold or dirt and –

Alexa, how does a human heart work?
How does a human heart work?

Blood is first received in the right atrium via
two veins, the vena cava superior and inferior –

Alexa, where do we go to when we die?
Where do we go to when we die?

Activating Google Maps. Completed activation.
Would you like to start from your current location?

Alexa, what does it mean to be alone?
What does it mean to be alone?

It is the silence left by words unsaid,
the cold expanse of half a bed.

It is the endless stretching of the hours,
the needless tending of plastic flowers.

It is an echo unanswered in a cave,
the fateful ping of the microwave.

It is the fraying of a worn shirt cuff,
and the howl – Alexa, stop! That's enough.

To My Excellent Lucasia, on Our Friendship
Katherine Philips

This poem explores the value of friendship.

I did not live until this time
    Crowned my felicity,
When I could say without a crime,
    I am not thine, but thee.

This carcass breathed, and walked, and slept,
    So that the world believed
There was a soul the motions kept;
    But they were all deceived.

For as a watch by art is wound
    To motion, such was mine:
But never had Orinda found
    A soul till she found thine;

Which now inspires, cures and supplies,
    And guides my darkened breast:
For thou art all that I can prize,
    My joy, my life, my rest.

No bridegroom's nor crown-conqueror's mirth
    To mine compared can be:
They have but pieces of the earth,
    I've all the world in thee.

Then let our flames still light and shine,
    And no false fear control,
As innocent as our design,
    Immortal as our soul.

Dancing Disk in the Sky
Hibaq Osman

The poem depicts the Moon's comforting, friendly presence in the sky.

If you asked what The Moon is
people would tell you
in their proudest voices:

The Moon is a circle in the sky
waiting for your greeting.
You should say hello
in any of the languages you know
or maybe say them all,
just in case!

The Moon is a reflection in the water
that jiggles with the wind.
It is a silver plate dancing with you
by the riverbank.

It has many friends
who speak to it at night
and you, with your small voice,
no need to worry
The Moon is a very good listener!

Look up and see,
if you peek behind your curtains
The Moon will dance for us
so nobody feels lonely.

On Forgetting That I Am a Tree LAMDA

Ruth Awolola

This poem uses the metaphor of a tree to contemplate finding a place in the world.

A poem in which I am growing.

A poem in which I am a tree,
And I am both appreciated and undervalued.

A poem in which I fear I did not dig into the past,
Did not think about my roots,
Forgot what it meant to be planted.

A poem in which I realise they may try to cut me down,
That I must change with the seasons,
That I do it so well
It looks like they are changing with me.

A poem in which I remember I have existed for centuries,
That centuries are far too small a unit of measurement,
That time found itself in the forests, woods and jungles.
Remember I have witnessed creation,
That I am key to it.

A poem in which some will carve their names into my skin
In hopes the universe will know them.
Where I am so tall I kiss the sun.
Trees cannot hide,
They belong to the day and to the night,
To the past and the future.

A poem in which I stop looking for it,
Because I am home.
I am habitat.
My branches are host and shelter
I am life-giver and fruit-bearer.
Self-sufficient protection.

A poem in which I remember I am a tree.

The Tiger
William Blake

This poem asks questions about belief and the presence of evil.

Tiger Tiger, burning bright
In the forests of the night,
What immortal hand or eye
Could frame thy fearful symmetry?

In what distant deeps or skies
Burnt the fire of thine eyes?
On what wings dare he aspire?
What the hand dare seize the fire?

And what shoulder and what art
Could twist the sinews of thy heart?
And, when thy heart began to beat,
What dread hand and what dread feet?

What the hammer? what the chain?
In what furnace was thy brain?
What the anvil? what dread grasp
Dare its deadly terrors clasp?

When the stars threw down their spears,
And watered heaven with their tears,
Did He smile His work to see?
Did He who made the lamb make thee?

Tiger, tiger, burning bright
In the forests of the night,
What immortal hand or eye
Dare frame thy fearful symmetry?

Voyage to the Bottom of My Bowl
Claudine Toutoungi

As this Speaker dives into a bowl of dumplings, they're amazed by the creatures they find.

I went deep-sea diving for dumplings
In a restaurant with my friends.
The chicken broth was superhot
And the seaweed gave me the bends.

I went deep sea diving for dumplings.
Full immersion was required.
I held my breath and plunged down low
To the sunken dumpling pile.

I swear an octopus passed me
And a cuttlefish tickled my cheek
But I kept my nerve and steered my course
Right down to the deepest deeps.

I chomped on a juicy morsel
Then up to the surface I rose –
Like a dolphin spouting sea-spray –
Chicken broth splurted out of my nose.

And my ears were bedecked with algae
And sea salt encrusted my eyes
And a customer yelled – *The Kraken awakes!*
I was quite the aquatic surprise.

The clientele screamed and fainted.
Some gasped. Some made for the door.
So I dipped back down for another lap
Round the shadowy, green sea floor.

And next time I went to the restaurant
I came prepared for the task
When the dumplings arrived, I popped on flippers
And a scuba-diving mask!

How to Cut a Pomegranate

Imtiaz Dharker

This poem uses pomegranate seeds to explore the connection with home.

'Never,' said my father,
'Never cut a pomegranate
through the heart. It will weep blood.
Treat it delicately, with respect.
Just slit the upper skin across four quarters.
This is a magic fruit,
so when you split it open, be prepared
for the jewels of the world to tumble out,
more precious than garnets,
more lustrous than rubies,
lit as if from inside.
Each jewel contains a living seed.
Separate one crystal.
Hold it up to catch the light.
Inside is a whole universe.
No common jewel can give you this.'
Afterwards, I tried to make necklaces
of pomegranate seeds.
The juice spurted out, bright crimson,
and stained my fingers, then my mouth.
I didn't mind. The juice tasted of gardens
I had never seen, voluptuous
with myrtle, lemon, jasmine,
and alive with parrots' wings.
The pomegranate reminded me
that somewhere I had another home.

A Boat Beneath a Sunny Sky

Lewis Carroll

This acrostic poem contemplates the passage time through the seasons and life.

A boat beneath a sunny sky,
Lingering onward dreamily
In an evening of July –

Children three that nestle near,
Eager eye and willing ear,
Pleased a simple tale to hear –

Long has paled that sunny sky:
Echoes fade and memories die.
Autumn frosts have slain July.

Still she haunts me, phantomwise,
Alice moving under skies
Never seen by waking eyes.

Children yet, the tale to hear,
Eager eye and willing ear,
Lovingly shall nestle near.

In a Wonderland they lie,
Dreaming as the days go by,
Dreaming as the summers die:

Ever drifting down the stream –
Lingering in the golden gleam –
Life, what is it but a dream?

Level 2 Speaking Verse and Prose: Grade 4 – Prose

Medusa

Jessie Burton

Medusa has been exiled to a remote island after being punished by the Gods. She has no human company and a head of snakes rather than a head of hair. In this section, Medusa reflects on the last four years of her life.

Four years previously, I'd had lovely hair. No – I should say: four years previously, everything had been different, and the very least of it was that I'd had lovely hair. But seeing as I've been accused of vanity enough times by people who nevertheless thought it their right to ogle me, I might as well tell you: my hair was lovely. I wore it long and unbound, except when fishing with my sisters, because you don't want hair in your eyes when you're trying to catch a squid. It was dark brown, it waved down my back, and my sisters would scent it with thyme oil.

I'd never thought about it much. It was just my hair. But I would come to miss it.

These days – from the nape of my neck, over the crown and right up to my forehead – my skull's a home for snakes. That's right. Snakes. Not a single strand of human hair, but yellow snakes and red snakes, green and blue and black snakes, snakes with spots on and snakes with stripes. A snake the colour of coral. Another one of silver. Three or four of brilliant gold. I'm a woman whose head hisses: quite the conversation starter, if there was anyone around to have a conversation.

No one in the world has a head like mine. At least, I don't think they do: I could be wrong. There could be women all over the world with snakes instead of hair. My sister Euryale thought they were a gift from the gods. While she had a point – it was literally the goddess Athena who did this to me – I begged to disagree. My creel of eels, my needy puppies; a head of fangs, excitable. Why would a young woman trying to get through her life want that?

When I breathed, I felt the snakes breathing too, and when I tensed my muscles they rose to strike. Euryale said that they were intelligent because I was, varied in colour and disposition because I was. They were unwieldy because I was, and, at times, disciplined because I was. Yet we were not quite in symbiosis, because despite all that, I couldn't always predict how they would behave. Four years together and I was still not entirely their mistress. They scared me.

I closed my eyes and tried not to think about Athena and her awful warning before we fled our home: Woe betide any man fool enough to look upon you

now! Athena hadn't hung around to explain herself further; shocked and sorrowful, we had fled soon after. I was still in the dark about what kind of woe she'd meant.

Chapter 2

Song Beneath the Tides

Beverley Birch

Set in East Africa, this novel follows Ally as she explores islands, beaches, coasts and creeks. In this section, Ally and her friends are exploring the island of Kisiri. They see bright purple lizards, blue butterflies and huge crocodiles, but they also feel a presence of something more mysterious.

Purple lizards watched them from a fallen tree, the island full of sound, trills and warbles and hums and clicks. Clouds of yellow birds floated among the palms.

The sun was hot, the air fragrant.

Already Ben was running between the bushes gleefully, jumping back with a shriek at a frantic scrabbling and a long body sliding away.

'A crocodile!'

'Lizard!' Huru flung his arms wide. 'Bigger than this!'

'Wow, it's brilliant. We could live here! Why's no one here?'

'No good water to drink.'

'But if we *brought* water, we could camp. Here!' Ben tore round in a circle, arms wide, marking the camp out.

Huru shook his head. 'No, we come all together, just for *Sherehe ya Kwazi* festival, when we thank Bwana Fumo and Mwana Zawati, singing, dancing, dancing, the whole night like this! Come, I show you where...' He ushered Ben and Jack into the trees.

Ally trailed behind with Leli.

Across the powder sand of the upper beach, between palms, among feathery ferny bushes. Trembling blue butterflies greeted them, a chirrup of birdsong, a well of sunlight in a circle of trees.

'Leli, are we near their burial place?' Ally whispered. 'You haven't told me properly about Fumo, yet. And I want to know all about Zawati.'

He gazed at her with a strangely pensive expression, and she wondered why. But he didn't explain, as if thinking something over.

'They are the first people of Shanza,' he began, as she reached the centre of the sunny glade. 'They have lost their mothers and fathers in a terrible killing time before. They escape terrible things. The big tides carry them from their burning city to Kisiri. They bring many others with them, to hide away in the mists. They stay one night, and when the sun is up they go across the water into the forest of the land, and after many months, when it is safe, they build Shanza.'

'Safe from what?'

A gust of wind plucks at her. Then she's holding her breath, as if the world holds its breath. As if she's alone, Leli gone.

She looks for him. She sees the clearing around her thronged with movement – a shifting of texture and shape, dark, flickering in the firelight. And murmuring sound, though is it just the wind stirring the palms?

She's held by the strangest idea: *if I move too fast, something will break, something will be lost.*

A touch on her shoulder – she's swayed slightly, almost a dizziness, and she turns to tell Leli it's all right, *I'm OK, really.*

Leli is too far away to have touched her.

Chapter 6

The Secret Garden
Frances Hodgson Burnett

Mary Lennox is sent to live in Yorkshire with her maternal uncle at Misselthwaite Manor. After arriving at the Manor, Mary discovers that the estate is home to a secret garden that belonged to her late aunt. In this section, she finally discovers where the garden is.

'You showed me where the key was yesterday,' she said. 'You ought to show me the door today; but I don't believe you know!'

The robin flew from his swinging spray of ivy on to the top of the wall and he opened his beak and sang a loud, lovely trill, merely to show off. Nothing in the world is quite as adorably lovely as a robin when he shows off – and they are nearly always doing it.

Mary Lennox had heard a great deal about Magic in her Ayah's stories, and she always said that what happened almost at that moment was Magic.

One of the nice little gusts of wind rushed down the walk, and it was a stronger one than the rest. It was strong enough to wave the branches of the trees, and it was more than strong enough to sway the trailing sprays of untrimmed ivy hanging from the wall. Mary had stepped close to the robin, and suddenly the gust of wind swung aside some loose ivy trails, and more suddenly still she jumped toward it and caught it in her hand. This she did because she had seen something under it – a round knob which had been covered by the leaves hanging over it. It was the knob of a door.

She put her hands under the leaves and began to pull and push them aside. Thick as the ivy hung, it nearly all was a loose and swinging curtain, though some had crept over wood and iron. Mary's heart began to thump and her hands to shake a little in her delight and excitement. The robin kept singing and twittering away and tilting his head on one side, as if he were as excited as she was. What was this under her hands which was square and made of iron and which her fingers found a hole in?

It was the lock of the door which had been closed ten years and she put her hand in her pocket, drew out the key and found it fitted the keyhole. She put the key in and turned it. It took two hands to do it, but it did turn.

And then she took a long breath and looked behind her up the long walk to see if any one was coming. No one was coming. No one ever did come, it seemed, and she took another long breath, because she could not help it, and she held back the swinging curtain of ivy and pushed back the door which opened slowly – slowly.

Then she slipped through it, and shut it behind her, and stood with her back against it, looking about her and breathing quite fast with excitement, and wonder, and delight.

She was standing *inside* the secret garden.

Chapter 8, 'The Robin Who Showed the Way'

The Cats We Meet Along The Way
Nadia Mikail

Time is running out for Aisha and her family. They recently discovered that the world is going to end due to an asteroid heading straight for earth. In this section, Aisha describes how they received the news.

The world found out it was ending on just another Tuesday.

IN A YEAR, the headlines screamed. Back when there had still been headlines. An asteroid heading straight for collision, Hollywood-perfect for the end of the world. It was really like something out of a movie. Sometimes it still felt like a cruel, extended prank.

When the news was announced, Aisha had been out with Walter on the beach, everything swathed in golden light, the waves coming in, going out, coming in again. They'd driven out for the weekend, phones left at home. They'd been laughing when people had started screaming. Then the beach had emptied like the tide rolling back, quick.

Aisha had thought: *tsunami*. She'd thought: *bombing, financial collapse, mass shooting*. Then they'd gotten into the car and driven home silently, and Esah had met them at the lime green front door and her face had been pale, her hands shaking. Aisha had realised it was all those things at once, and the end of all those things at once.

Here was how the end of the world was predicted to play out:

The world wreathed in fire and smoke, everything burning.

Earthquakes and tsunamis shuddering, cracking, shifting what was left.

Volcanoes erupting, water corrosive, the very air poison, and what was left dark, the sun sheathed in unlight.

It turned out that governments had known about it for four years, and planned everything from deflecting the path of the asteroid, to frantically focusing their efforts on space, to attempting to build large underground bunkers – but when none of it seemed like it was going to work, they had all addressed their people at the same time.

These times are dark, the speeches all started, *but one thing is to be remembered: the power of humanity to come together and face what is to come is undefeated.* Most of the world had watched the broadcast, a video that had popped up while they were scrolling through their timeline or across their screen during their nightly binge-watch. Some people heard it on the radio, and some on their smartwatches. Some people had woken up to the news.

Most people immediately started digging bunkers or building shelters. Scientists came on the news to say that even the strongest ones wouldn't be much use against an asteroid miles-wide, trust them, they'd checked. They teleconferenced in from all over the world: *Spend time with your loved ones. Make the most of what's left. Say your prayers.* Their faces had been set and resigned, their opinions reasoned and fact-checked: they were the few who had spent years desperately scrabbling, after all.

'An Explanation (four months ago)'

Pride and Prejudice

Jane Austen

Elizabeth Bennet lives at the family estate in Hertfordshire. Elizabeth Bennet meets Mr Darcy at the Netherfield party, where he dismisses her on the grounds that she is 'not handsome enough'. Whilst Elizabeth is incredibly offended, the pair find themselves drawn to each other again and again. In this section, Elizabeth and Mr Darcy dance.

The two first dances, however, brought a return of distress: they were dances of mortification. Mr Collins, awkward and solemn, apologizing instead of attending, and often moving wrong without being aware of it, gave her all the shame and misery which a disagreeable partner for a couple of dances can give. The moment of her release from him was ecstasy.

She danced next with an officer, and had the refreshment of talking of Wickham, and of hearing that he was universally liked. When those dances were over, she returned to Charlotte Lucas, and was in conversation with her, when she found herself suddenly addressed by Mr Darcy, who took her so much by surprise in his application for her hand, that, without knowing what she did, she accepted him. He walked away again immediately, and she was left to fret over her own want of presence of mind: Charlotte tried to console her.

'I dare say you will find him very agreeable.'

'Heaven forbid! That would be the greatest misfortune of all! To find a man agreeable whom one is determined to hate! Do not wish me such an evil.'

When the dancing recommenced, however, and Darcy approached to claim her hand, Charlotte could not help cautioning her, in a whisper, not to be a simpleton, and allow her fancy for Wickham to make her appear unpleasant in the eyes of a man ten times his consequence. Elizabeth made no answer, and took her place in the set, amazed at the dignity to which she was arrived in being allowed to stand opposite to Mr Darcy, and reading in her neighbours' looks their equal amazement in beholding it. They stood for some time without speaking a word; and she began to imagine that their silence was to last through the two dances, and, at first, was resolved not to break it; till suddenly fancying that it would be the greater punishment to her partner to oblige him to talk, she made some slight observation on the dance. He replied, and was again silent. After a pause of some minutes, she addressed him a second time, with –

'It is your turn to say something now, Mr Darcy. I talked about the dance, and you ought to make some kind of remark on the size of the room, or the number of couples.'

He smiled, and assured her that whatever she wished him to say should be said.

'Very well; that reply will do for the present. Perhaps, by-and-by, I may observe that private balls are much pleasanter than public ones; but now we may be silent.'

Chapter 18

The Beast Player

Nahoko Uehashi, translated by **Cathy Hirano**

When Elin's mother is sentenced to death, her final act is to send Elin far away from home for safety. Elin is taken in by a beekeeper named Joeun. In this section, Joeun has made the bees a new beehive, which Elin finds curious.

Elin looked at the box. Bees were crawling in and out of the hive, and many more were flying about in agitation. They had flown off in search of a new home. Wouldn't they run away rather than be shut up in a box once again so close by? They might be enjoying the sugar water right now, but once it was gone, wouldn't they leave?

Joeun put a hand on her shoulder. 'If it bothers you that much, why don't you stay and watch? I'll go back to the house and call you when lunch is ready. But you'd better come when I call... And don't go near that box.'

Elin nodded. Once he had left, everything seemed suddenly very quiet. There was only the sound of the breeze rustling the branches and the bees humming. She watched them move. Then suddenly her eyes opened wide. The bees that had been flitting back and forth around the box began to drop toward it, one after the other, as if drawn by a magnet. When they reached the entrance, they folded their wings and streamed inside, as if to say, 'We're home.' Before she knew it, not a bee was left. She stared at the box, spellbound. This, she thought, was true magic. What on earth could they be doing in there? They had set off on a journey to a new land. Were they now consoling each other, saying, 'I guess this place will have to do'? And how did that huge black swarm fit in there? She longed to peek inside...

Joeun had told her not to go near the hive. But as long as she didn't touch it, if she just peeked inside that opening without startling the bees, perhaps she could see something. She glanced behind her and then moved stealthily toward the box. It was very quiet. She crouched down and peered inside the long narrow slit that served as an entrance. It was so dark that she could not see anything. Or maybe she could. Something was moving. Was it bees? She could hear a whirring of wings. What were they doing?

She tilted her head and strained her eyes, trying to see inside when suddenly someone grabbed her shoulder. Startled, she was about to scream when a large hand covered her mouth, and she found herself tucked under an arm and

carried away. Joeun did not set her down until he reached the house. 'I told you not to go near that box!'

Part 1, 'The Toda'; Chapter 1, 'The Beekeeper. 3: Royal Jelly'

The Red-Headed League (The Adventures of Sherlock Holmes)
Arthur Conan Doyle

Sherlock Holmes and John Watson are on a quest to solve the mystery of the 'Red-Headed League', an organisation that works only with red-headed men. Jabez Wilson previously worked for the Red-Headed League, but approaches Holmes and Watson after the organisation is mysteriously dissolved. Holmes suspects that a crime is about to be committed.

What a time it seemed! From comparing notes afterwards it was but an hour and a quarter, yet it appeared to me that the night must have almost gone, and the dawn be breaking above us. My limbs were weary and stiff, for I feared to change my position; yet my nerves were worked up to the highest pitch of tension, and my hearing was so acute that I could not only hear the gentle breathing of my companions, but I could distinguish the deeper, heavier in-breath of the bulky Jones from the thin, sighing note of the bank director. From my position I could look over the case in the direction of the floor. Suddenly my eyes caught the glint of a light.

At first it was but a lurid spark upon the stone pavement. Then it lengthened out until it became a yellow line, and then, without any warning or sound, a gash seemed to open and a hand appeared; a white, almost womanly hand, which felt about in the centre of the little area of light. For a minute or more the hand, with its writhing fingers, protruded out of the floor. Then it was withdrawn as suddenly as it appeared, and all was dark again save the single lurid spark which marked a chink between the stones.

Its disappearance, however, was but momentary. With a rending, tearing sound, one of the broad, white stones turned over upon its side, and left a square, gaping hole, through which streamed the light of a lantern. Over the edge there peeped a clean-cut, boyish face, which looked keenly about it, and then, with a hand on either side of the aperture, drew itself shoulder-high and waist-high, until one knee rested upon the edge. In another instant he stood at the side of the hole, and was hauling after him a companion, lithe and small like himself, with a pale face and a shock of very red hair.

'It's all clear,' he whispered. 'Have you the chisel and the bags. Great Scott! Jump, Archie, jump, and I'll swing for it!'

Sherlock Holmes had sprung out and seized the intruder by the collar. The other dived down the hole, and I heard the sound of rending cloth as Jones

clutched at his skirts. The light flashed upon the barrel of a revolver, but Holmes's hunting crop came down on the man's wrist, and the pistol clinked upon the stone floor.

'It's no use, John Clay,' said Holmes, blandly. 'You have no chance at all.'

The Heart of Happy Hollow
Paul Laurence Dunbar

It is 1985 and Bud is part of the Cadets. His team are competing in the end of year drills at school. Bud's Company is the favourite to win, but things do not go to plan. To his dismay, Bud drops the bayonet, and his dreams come tumbling down.

'They are doing splendidly, they'll win, they'll win yet in spite of the second volley.'

Company 'A', in columns of fours, had executed the right oblique in double time, and halted amid cheers; then formed left halt into line without halting. The next movement was one looked forward to with much anxiety on account of its difficulty. The order was marching by fours to fix or unfix bayonets. They were going at a quick step, but the boys' hands were steady – hope was bright in their hearts. They were doing it rapidly and freely, when suddenly from the ranks there was the bright gleam of steel lower down than it should have been. A gasp broke from the breasts of Company 'A's' friends. The blue and white drooped disconsolately, while a few heartless ones who wore other colours attempted to hiss. Someone had dropped his bayonet. But with muscles unquivering, without a turned head, the company moved on as if nothing had happened, while one of the judges, an army officer, stepped into the wake of the boys and picked up the fallen steel.

No two eyes had seen half so quickly as Hannah and Little Sister's who the blunderer was. In the whole drill there had been but one figure for them, and that was Bud, Bud, and it was he who had dropped his bayonet. Anxious, nervous with the desire to please them, perhaps with a shade too much of thought of them looking on with their hearts in their eyes, he had fumbled, and lost all that he was striving for. His head went round and round and all seemed black before him.

He executed the movements in a dazed way. The applause, generous and sympathetic, as his company left the parade ground, came to him from afar off, and like a wounded animal he crept away from his comrades, not because their reproaches stung him, for he did not hear them, but because he wanted to think what his mother and 'Little Sister' would say, but his misery was as nothing to that of the two who sat up there amid the ranks of the blue and white holding each other's hands with a despairing grip. To Bud all of the rest of the contest was a horrid nightmare; he hardly knew when the three companies

were marched back to receive the judges' decision. The applause that greeted Company 'B' when the blue ribbons were pinned on the members' coats meant nothing to his ears. He had disgraced himself and his company. What would his mother and his 'Little Sister' say?

Chapter 16, 'The Boy and the Bayonet'

Level 2 Speaking Verse and Prose: Grade 5 – Verse

Wild Geese

Mary Oliver

This poem explores the importance of being kind to yourself.

You do not have to be good.
You do not have to walk on your knees
for a hundred miles through the desert repenting.
You only have to let the soft animal of your body
love what it loves.
Tell me about despair, yours, and I will tell you mine.
Meanwhile the world goes on.
Meanwhile the sun and the clear pebbles of the rain
are moving across the landscapes,
over the prairies and the deep trees,
the mountains and the rivers.
Meanwhile the wild geese, high in the clean blue air,
are heading home again.
Whoever you are, no matter how lonely,
the world offers itself to your imagination,
calls to you like the wild geese, harsh and exciting –
over and over announcing your place
in the family of things.

I Wandered Lonely as a Cloud
William Wordsworth

This poem depicts an emotional connection to the natural world.

I wandered lonely as a cloud
That floats on high o'er vales and hills,
When all at once I saw a crowd,
A host, of golden daffodils;
Beside the lake, beneath the trees,
Fluttering and dancing in the breeze.

Continuous as the stars that shine
And twinkle on the milky way,
They stretched in never-ending line
Along the margin of a bay:
Ten thousand saw I at a glance,
Tossing their heads in sprightly dance.

The waves beside them danced; but they
Out-did the sparkling waves in glee:
A poet could not but be gay,
In such a jocund company:
I gazed – and gazed – but little thought
What wealth the show to me had brought:

For oft, when on my couch I lie
In vacant or in pensive mood,
They flash upon that inward eye
Which is the bliss of solitude;
And then my heart with pleasure fills,
And dances with the daffodils.

The Sky is Too Wide for Two Birds to Collide

Kareem Parkins-Brown

This poem addresses the personified sky with a series of questions.

Oi, sky, I have a question.
What is it like flossing pigeons out of your teeth?
Why are you everywhere for no reason?
     What's it like to be nothing but a face?
Did you and the ocean ever swap positions
     so that it made more sense when it rained?

Sky, I have a request
since you have so much face
would you tattoo my dead friend under your eye?
You know the devil landed where I'm standing?
     You can put the sun back in your bag and call it off.

If earth does turn out to be flat, you reckon our egos will follow?
Aren't we nothing but a frisbee travelling towards some happy golden retriever?

Hey sky, we should compromise, say the earth is squashed
because that suggests you would be down here with us?
Me and my cousins could reach up,
itch that spot that's been bugging you for years.
That spot too wide for two birds to collide.

George Moses Horton, Myself

George Moses Horton

This poem presents a Speaker who is inspired to learn, grow and find freedom.

I feel myself in need
  Of the inspiring strains of ancient lore,
My heart to lift, my empty mind to feed,
  And all the world explore.

I know that I am old
  And never can recover what is past,
But for the future may some light unfold
  And soar from ages blast.

I feel resolved to try,
  My wish to prove, my calling to pursue,
Or mount up from the earth into the sky,
  To show what Heaven can do.

My genius from a boy,
  Has fluttered like a bird within my heart;
But could not thus confined her powers employ,
  Impatient to depart.

She like a restless bird,
  Would spread her wing, her power to be unfurl'd,
And let her songs be loudly heard,
  And dart from world to world.

Front Door

Imtiaz Dharker

*This poem shows the changes when moving between home and the world
outside.*

Wherever I have lived,
walking out of the front door
every morning
means crossing over
to a foreign country.
One language inside the house,
another out.
The food and clothes
and customs change.
The fingers on my hand turn
into forks.
I call it adaptation
when my tongue switches
from one grammar to another,
but the truth is I'm addicted now,
high on the rush
of daily displacement,
speeding to a different time zone,
heading into altered weather,
landing as another person.
Don't think I haven't noticed
you're on the same trip too.

Fear

Kahlil Gibran

This poem uses the imagery of a river to explore risk and fear.

It is said that before entering the sea
a river trembles with fear.

She looks back at the path she has travelled,
from the peaks of the mountains,
the long winding roads crossing forests and villages.

And in front of her,
she sees an ocean so vast,
that to enter
there seems nothing more than to disappear forever.

But there is no other way.
The river can not go back.

Nobody can go back.
To go back is impossible in existence.

The river needs to take the risk
of entering the ocean
because only then will fear disappear,
because that's where the river will know
it's not about disappearing into the ocean,
but of becoming the ocean.

The Naming of Cats

T. S. Eliot

This poem presents different names we have for cats, and those they reserve for themselves.

The Naming of Cats is a difficult matter,
    It isn't just one of your holiday games;
You may think at first I'm as mad as a hatter
When I tell you, a cat must have THREE DIFFERENT NAMES.
First of all, there's the name that the family use daily,
    Such as Peter, Augustus, Alonzo, or James,
Such as Victor or Jonathan, George or Bill Bailey –
    All of them sensible everyday names.
There are fancier names if you think they sound sweeter,
    Some for the gentlemen, some for the dames:
Such as Plato, Admetus, Electra, Demeter –
    But all of them sensible everyday names,
But I tell you, a cat needs a name that's particular,
    A name that's peculiar, and more dignified,
Else how can he keep up his tail perpendicular,
    Or spread out his whiskers, or cherish his pride?
Of names of this kind, I can give you a quorum,
    Such as Munkustrap, Quaxo, or Coricopat,
Such as Bombalurina, or else Jellylorum –
    Names that never belong to more than one cat.
But above and beyond there's still one name left over,
    And that is the name that you never will guess;
The name that no human research can discover –
    But THE CAT HIMSELF KNOWS, and will never confess.
When you notice a cat in profound meditation,
    The reason, I tell you, is always the same:
His mind is engaged in a rapt contemplation
    Of the thought, of the thought, of the thought of his name:
        His ineffable effable
        Effanineffable
Deep and inscrutable singular name.

Street Cries

Sarojini Naidu

This poem depicts a normal day in India, through the morning, afternoon and night.

When dawn's first cymbals beat upon the sky,
Rousing the world to labour's various cry,
To tend the flock, to bind the mellowing grain,
From ardent toil to forge a little gain,
And fasting men go forth on hurrying feet,
BUY BREAD, BUY BREAD, rings down the eager street.

When the earth falters and the waters swoon
With the implacable radiance of noon,
And in dim shelters koils hush their notes,
And the faint, thirsting blood in languid throats
Craves liquid succour from the cruel heat,
BUY FRUIT, BUY FRUIT, steals down the panting street.

When twilight twinkling o'er the gay bazaars,
Unfurls a sudden canopy of stars,
When lutes are strung and fragrant torches lit
On white roof-terraces where lovers sit
Drinking together of life's poignant sweet,
BUY FLOWERS, BUY FLOWERS, floats down the singing street.

Level 2 Speaking Verse and Prose: Grade 5 – Prose

Attention Seekers

Emma Brankin

Ash and Jenna recently ended their relationship. Ash keeps their cat and gives it an Instagram page, where its fluffy tail and sassy personality prove popular. In this section, the cat gets a surprising new follower.

The cat surpasses Ash in Instagram followers. She tells herself she doesn't mind, but she does. Gone is that flighty fluttering of validation in her chest whenever her phone buzzes. Now, the likes, the comments, and follows are almost never for her. Even the most recent post - of the cat's tail - is proving infuriatingly popular.

She sighs. Over on her personal account, there is an underwhelming response to her recent upload. Thirty-four likes. The cat could get that many likes just coughing up a photo of a furball.

She types 'Jenna' into her search bar. As the profile loads, air jams in her chest but the same sight greets her: Blocked.

The cat enters the living room. Ash reaches out a welcoming hand but its eyes narrow as it looks away. This is nothing new. The cat, despite being unaware of its burgeoning celebrity status, has always had the ego and entitlement of a Kardashian. The animal dumps its black, furry backside onto the carpet, unfurls a leg like a pole dancer and, with a Barbie-pink tongue, begins licking its crotch.

Her phone buzzes with comments about the tail:

SooOOooOOoo fluffy.

Swish swish bish.

Feather boa fierceness.

Ash scowls. She's cultivating a charming presence online for the cat, but, like a stage-mother, lip curling while clutching a vodka martini in the wings, she's growing to resent her ungrateful offspring.

She bats one of the cat's toys towards it. The animal watches as the ball travels beyond its reach. Its disinterest is palpable. Then, for reasons only known to itself, it decides to chirrup, twist onto its back and writhe shamelessly. Ash

dutifully switches on her phones camera and starts snapping. She then spends the next thirty minutes deciding which filter best accentuates the animal's emerald-flecked eyes.

Then, something incredible happens. Dazed, she holds out her phone as if to show her cat her screen. She reads the notifications aloud, every word soaked in incredulity.

'Jenna has liked your image.'

It appears Ash's ex has chosen to keep in contact with the cat.

Jenna likes five more pictures on the cat's account over the next few days. Ash screen grabs everything and conducts hourly social media autopsies about what it all might mean. She obsesses forensically over the nature of the photos her ex singles out, the times of day the interactions occur, the rate of her liking. Ash's uploads become more frequent. Captions more pointed. Posts with the cat in front of the television watching *their* favourite programme. The cat curled on top of the jumper Jenna left behind. The cat snoozing in the bathroom sink, with Ash's reflection, face fully made up, clearly visible in the mirror above it.

Story 5, 'Caturday'

Great Expectations

Charles Dickens

Orphaned boy Pip is on a journey to become an educated gentleman. When Pip was a young boy, he was accosted by a convict who demanded food and a file from him. Years later, the convict approaches Pip again. Just before this section, Pip learns that the convict is secretly the benefactor of his inheritance.

Miss Havisham's intentions towards me, all a mere dream; Estella not designed for me; I only suffered in Satis House as a convenience, a sting for the greedy relations, a model with a mechanical heart to practise on when no other practice was at hand; those were the first smarts I had. But, sharpest and deepest pain of all, – it was for the convict, guilty of I knew not what crimes, and liable to be taken out of those rooms where I sat thinking, and hanged at the Old Bailey door, that I had deserted Joe.

I would not have gone back to Joe now, I would not have gone back to Biddy now, for any consideration; simply, I suppose, because my sense of my own worthless conduct to them was greater than every consideration. No wisdom on earth could have given me the comfort that I should have derived from their simplicity and fidelity; but I could never, never, undo what I had done.

In every rage of wind and rush of rain, I heard pursuers. Twice, I could have sworn there was a knocking and whispering at the outer door. With these fears upon me, I began either to imagine or recall that I had had mysterious warnings of this man's approach. That, for weeks gone by, I had passed faces in the streets which I had thought like his. That these likenesses had grown more numerous, as he, coming over the sea, had drawn near. That his wicked spirit had somehow sent these messengers to mine, and that now on this stormy night he was as good as his word, and with me.

Crowding up with these reflections came the reflection that I had seen him with my childish eyes to be a desperately violent man; that I had heard that other convict reiterate that he had tried to murder him; that I had seen him down in the ditch tearing and fighting like a wild beast. Out of such remembrances I brought into the light of the fire a half-formed terror that it might not be safe to be shut up there with him in the dead of the wild solitary night. This dilated until it filled the room, and impelled me to take a candle and go in and look at my dreadful burden.

He had rolled a handkerchief round his head, and his face was set and lowering in his sleep. But he was asleep, and quietly too, though he had a pistol lying on this pillow. Assured of this, I softly removed the key to the outside of his door, and turned it on him before I again sat down by the fire. Gradually I slipped from the chair and lay on the floor.

Chapter 39

Amari and the Night Brothers

B. B. Alston

Amari has joined the Bureau of Supernatural Affairs, a world of mermaids, aliens and weredragons. Amari has her own secret power: she is a magician. Here, Amari puts on a magic show.

'Habitat,' I continue. And I paint an illusion, letting the image pour out of my fingertips. Suddenly, the auditorium looks like a street in my neighbourhood. A few people gasp, some keep turning their heads back and forth while others reach out with their hands to see if they can touch anything. 'I've lived in the Rosewood Projects for as long as I can remember. It's basically a low-income apartment complex for people who need a little help getting by. People joke and call it the 'hood or the bad side of town, but it's full of good people if you give them a chance'.

I change the illusion to my apartment and have the audience glide through like one of those virtual house tours on the internet. 'This is home for me. It's probably not much compared to where a lot of you guys live, but it's all I've ever known. This is my room, junky as always. And this is where the famous Agent Quinton Peters used to sleep when he was just my big brother. We would lie in here and dream about the things we were going to do. He made me believe I could actually do anything I set my mind to. He made me believe in me'.

'Hobbies. Well, usually I compete in the summer swim meets at the rec centre but I got a little busy this year trying to make Junior Agent.' My joke gets a few laughs, and it's enough to encourage me to keep going.

'Go to the Department of Undersea Relations,' someone shouts.

'Oh, good point,' I say. 'Guess it's hard to complain about missing the pool when there's a whole floor that's underwater.'

That gets even more laughs.

'I also like to read books. The fun ones, not *Supernatural Laws & Regulations*. That author should definitely be investigated for crimes against good moods and staying awake. I'd much rather read books about magic and adventure – though I never imagined my own life would ever come close! Recently I've taken up another hobby, and that's practising magic, which is mostly just me playing

around with illusions.' I flash an image of Elsie freaking out that time I turned her hair pink.

'I think I've got pretty good. Tell me what you guys think...'

And then I put on a show. I turn the ceiling into a cloudless starry night sky and let the aurora borealis glimmer just beyond their fingertips as shooting stars zip across the auditorium. I turn the room dark again, and suddenly fireworks explode and sparkle overhead one after the other.

Chapter 28

Little Men: Life at Plumfield with Jo's Boys
Louisa May Alcott

Mrs Josephine Bhaer and her husband run Plumfield School, which is full of mischievous young children. In this section, Rob and Nan decide to go on an adventure when picking Huckleberries, but there's trouble round the corner: they're lost.

But of all the adventures that happened on this afternoon that which befell Nan and Rob was the most exciting, and it long remained one of the favorite histories of the household. Having explored the country pretty generally, torn three rents in her frock, and scratched her face in a barberry-bush, Nan began to pick the berries that shone like big, black beads on the low, green bushes. Her nimble fingers flew, but still her basket did not fill up as rapidly as she desired, so she kept wandering here and there to search for better places, instead of picking contentedly and steadily as Daisy did. Rob followed Nan, for her energy suited him better than his cousin's patience, and he too was anxious to have the biggest and best berries for Marmar.

'I keep putting 'em in, but it don't fill up, and I'm so tired,' said Rob, pausing a moment to rest his short legs, and beginning to think huckleberrying was not all his fancy painted it; for the sun blazed, Nan skipped hither and thither like a grasshopper, and the berries fell out of his pail almost as fast as he put them in, because, in his struggles with the bushes, it was often upside-down.

'Last time we came they were ever so much thicker over that wall – great bouncers; and there is a cave there, where the boys made a fire. Let's go and fill our things quick, and then hide in the cave and let the others find us,' proposed Nan, thirsting for adventures.

Rob consented, and away they went, scrambling over the wall and running down the sloping fields on the other side, till they were hidden among the rocks and underbrush. The berries were thick, and at last the pails were actually full. It was shady and cool down there, and a little spring gave the thirsty children a refreshing drink out of its mossy cup.

'Now we will go and rest in the cave, and eat our lunch,' said Nan, well satisfied with her success so far.

'Do you know the way?' asked Rob.

'Course I do; I've been once, and I always remember. Didn't I go and get my box all right?'

That convinced Rob, and he followed blindly as Nan led him over stock and stone, and brought him, after much meandering, to a small recess in the rock, where the blackened stones showed that fires had been made.

'Now, isn't it nice?' asked Nan, as she took out a bit of bread-and-butter, rather damaged by being mixed up with nails, fish-hooks, stones and other foreign substances, in the young lady's pocket.

'Yes; do you think they will find us soon?' asked Rob, who found the shadowy glen rather dull, and began to long for more society.

'No, I don't; because if I hear them, I shall hide, and have fun making them find me.'

Chapter 12, 'Huckleberries'

Six of Crows
Leigh Bardugo

In the fictional world of Ketterdam, Kez Brekker and his crew attempt to pull off an ambitious heist. Part of his crew are Nina and Matthias, who have a complicated friendship and history. Once in love but then brutally betrayed by Nina, Matthias is compelled to expose her actions.

'No, Nina,' Matthias said. 'Tell them. You said you were my friend once. Do you remember?' He turned to the others. 'We travelled together for three weeks. I saved her life. We saved each other. When we got to Elling, we... I could have revealed her to the soldiers we saw there at any time. But I didn't.' Matthias started pacing, his voice rising, as if the memories were getting the better of him. 'I borrowed money. I arranged lodging. I was willing to betray everything I believed in for the sake of her safety. When I saw her down to the docks so we could try to book passage, there was a Kerch trader there, ready to set sail.' Matthias was there again, standing on the docks with her, she could see it in his eyes. 'Ask her what she did then, this honourable ally, this girl who stands in judgement of me and my kind.'

No one said a word, but they were watching, waiting.

'*Tell them*, Nina,' he demanded. 'They should know how you treat your friends.'

Nina swallowed, then forced herself to meet their gazes. 'I told the Kerch that he was a slaver and that he'd taken me prisoner. I threw myself on their mercy and begged them to help me. I had a seal I'd taken from a slaving ship we'd raided near the Wandering Isle. I used it as proof.'

She couldn't bear to look at them. Kaz knew, of course. She'd had to tell him the charges she'd made and tried recant when she was begging for his assistance. But Kaz had never probed, never asked why, never chastised her. In a way, telling Kaz had been a comfort. There could be no judgement from a boy known as Dirtyhands.

But now the truth was there for everyone to see. Privately, the Kerch knew slaves moved in and out of the ports of Ketterdam, and most indentures were really slaves by another name. But publicly, they reviled it and were obligated to prosecute all slavers. Nina had known exactly what would happen when she'd branded Matthais with the charge.

'I didn't understand what was happening,' said Matthias. 'I didn't speak Kerch, but Nina certainly did. They seized me and put me in chains. They tossed me in the brig and kept me there in the dark for weeks while we crossed the sea. The next time I saw daylight was when they led me off the ship in Ketterdam.'

'I had no choice,' Nina said, the ache of tears pressing at her throat. 'You don't know –'

'Just tell me one thing,' he said. There was anger in his voice, but she could hear something else, too, a kind of pleading. 'If you could go back, if you could undo what you did to me, would you?'

Chapter 20, 'Nina'

The Yellow Wallpaper

Charlotte Perkins Gilman

When a woman is confined to one room in an old mansion, her mental health deteriorates. She begins to believe that there is a woman trapped inside the patterns on the wallpaper. This section is an insight into her mind.

Then I peeled off all the paper I could reach standing on the floor. It sticks horribly and the pattern just enjoys it! All those strangled heads and bulbous eyes and waddling fungus growths just shriek with derision!

I am getting angry enough to do something desperate. To jump out of the window would be admirable exercise, but the bars are too strong even to try.

Besides I wouldn't do it. Of course not. I know well enough that a step like that is improper and might be misconstrued.

I don't like to *look* out of the windows even – there are so many of those creeping women, and they creep so fast.

I wonder if they all come out of that wallpaper as I did?

But I am securely fastened now by my well-hidden rope – you don't get *me* out in the road there!

I suppose I shall have to get back behind the pattern when it comes night, and that is hard!

It is so pleasant to be out in this great room and creep around as I please!

I don't want to go outside. I won't, even if Jennie asks me to.

For outside you have to creep on the ground, and everything is green instead of yellow.

But here I can creep smoothly on the floor, and my shoulder just fits in that long smooch around the wall, so I cannot lose my way.

Why, there's John at the door!

It is no use, young man, you can't open it!

How he does call and pound!

Now he's crying for an axe.

It would be a shame to break down that beautiful door!

'John dear!' said I in the gentlest voice, 'the key is down by the front steps, under a plantain leaf!'

That silenced him for a few moments.

Then he said – very quietly indeed, 'Open the door, my darling!'

'I can't,' said I. 'The key is down by the front door under a plantain leaf!'

And then I said it again, several times, very gently and slowly, and said it so often that he had to go and see, and he got it, of course, and came in. He stopped short by the door.

'What is the matter?' he cried. 'For God's sake, what are you doing!'

I kept on creeping just the same, but I looked at him over my shoulder.

'I've got out at last,' said I, 'in spite of you and Jane! And I've pulled off most of the paper, so you can't put me back!'

Now why should that man have fainted? But he did, and right across my path by the wall, so that I had to creep over him every time!

The Three Musketeers

Alexandre Dumas and **Auguste Maquet**

D'Artagnan has left his home for Paris, with the intention of making his fortune. Through a series of blunders, D'Artagnan finds himself with three duels to fight: with Athos at noon, with Porthos at one o'clock and with Aramis at two o'clock. In this section, D'Artagnan rushes to the duelling spot, whilst assessing how to approach each of his opponents.

D'Artagnan was acquainted with nobody in Paris. He went therefore to his appointment with Athos without a second, determined to be satisfied with those his adversary should choose. Besides, his intention was formed to make the brave Musketeer all suitable apologies, but without meanness or weakness, fearing that might result from this duel which generally results from an affair of this kind, when a young and vigorous man fights with an adversary who is wounded and weakened – if conquered, he doubles the triumph of his antagonist; if a conqueror, he is accused of foul play and want of courage.

Now, we must have badly painted the character of our adventure seeker, or our readers must have already perceived that D'Artagnan was not an ordinary man; therefore, while repeating to himself that his death was inevitable, he did not make up his mind to die quietly, as one less courageous and less restrained might have done in his place. He reflected upon the different characters of those with whom he was going to fight, and began to view his situation more clearly. He hoped, by means of loyal excuses, to make a friend of Athos, whose lordly air and austere bearing pleased him much. He flattered himself he should be able to frighten Porthos with the adventure of the baldric, which he might, if not killed upon the spot, relate to everybody a recital which, well managed, would cover Porthos with ridicule. As to the astute Aramis, he did not entertain much dread of him; and supposing he should be able to get so far, he determined to dispatch him in good style or at least, by hitting him in the face, as Cæsar recommended his soldiers do to those of Pompey, to damage forever the beauty of which he was so proud.

In addition to this, D'Artagnan possessed that invincible stock of resolution which the counsels of his father had implanted in his heart: 'Endure nothing from anyone but the king, the cardinal, and Monsieur de Tréville.' He flew, then, rather than walked, toward the convent of the Carmes Déchaussés, or rather Deschaux, as it was called at that period, a sort of building without a window, surrounded by barren fields – an accessory to the Preaux-Clercs, and which was generally employed as the place for the duels of men who had no time to lose.

Chapter 5, 'The King's Musketeers and the Cardinal's Guards'

Tsunami Girl

Julian Sedgwick and **Chie Kutsuwada**

Yūki has gone to live with her grandfather in Japan, who is a Manga artist and encourages Yūki's art and imagination. However, during her visit, their home is hit by the East Coast Earthquake and Tsunami. This section describes the devastation of the tsunami's initial impact.

She tries to shout for Grandpa again, but all the air has gone from her lungs. Tries to will her legs to move, but it's as if they are stuck to the ground. And try as she might it's impossible to pull her eyes from the ocean.

The exposed sea bed looks so strange, so otherworldly, so impossible. Beyond that, one of the boats is still visible, motionless on the water some three or four kilometres out now. But then – horribly – it seems to lift up, and up, and hang high in what seconds ago was air, floating impossibly, then suddenly disappearing as if it has winked out of existence.

It's coming.

Not a disaster movie tidal wave, just a vast swell on the sea like a dark mountain ridge – it must be dozens of metres tall – and it's coming, the tsunami is coming.

Yūki raises the whistle to her mouth, takes a huge breath and blows as hard as she can. Nothing. Just a fluttering, wheezy sound. She shakes it hard and then tries again, fingers trembling as she holds it to her dry lips, her rapid heartbeat chopping away in her ears.

Not a peep, the stupid thing must be bust.

One more soundless blow, and a second later she is sliding, running, slipping down the steep path, bellowing, 'GRANDPA! GRANDPA!' over and over again at the top of her lungs. She stumbles in the soft earth, and a branch slashes her face, leaving a hot line on her cheek, knocking her glasses askew. Grabbing a tree trunk to stop the freefall, she clings to it for a few seconds, pushing the glasses back into place, and glances back out to see where the wave has reached.

There's a great puff of white that at first she takes to be smoke, erupting all along the line where the furthest houses and pines mark the coast. But it's not smoke, it's a long, foaming mess of water and spray hitting the land proper, detonating over the sea wall, the dunes, the trees, smashing anything in its path, obliterating everything. A moment later the noise follows: low and ominous, like a wall of thunder filling the air as the water crushes the shore and starts to eat across the flat land towards her, into and over houses, foam churning above its thick black body as it slams into the elementary school, swamping it to the height of the roof in seconds. Caught in the wave she glimpses a small white car, then something else, square and boxy. A shed? No, something bigger: a small house – a house! – splintering to bits even as she recognises what it is, and all of it, all the black water and white thundering wave crest, seems to pick up speed, the sound getting louder and louder and louder.

Chapter 8, 'The Thousand-Year Wave'

Level 3 Speaking Verse and Prose: Grade 6 – Verse

If We Remain Civil and Obedient Now

Nikita Gill

This poem challenges cruelty, oppression and complicity.

They will ask us in the future how it happened,
who allowed it, how could we just ignore it
when it stormed in so loudly,
like a thunderous beast,
could we not hear it?
This half beast half demon sitting
outside our doors, growling,
baring teeth, ready to rip out
the throats of whole people
erase the marginalized,
rip into the bones of the vulnerable,
why did we just sit there and watch
helplessly, asking no questions,
show them the evidence of
the thunderous applause
each act of cruelty is greeted with,
show them the raucous laughter
with which they celebrate the pain
each marginalized person feels
as their rights and liberties are taken.

Let them see for themselves
The bare bones of truth
until they realise, like us, horrified,
'The cruelty was the point.
My God, the cruelty was the point'.

He Thinks of his Past Faces

John Canfield

This poem reflects on life and the lessons it teaches.

When I was growing up I had a trait,
every time a camera was produced
to take a family snap: I'd stand up straight,
then cheeks and lips and tongue were quickly loosed

into a silly face, a gurn; my eyes
rolled in to both point at my wrinkled nose;
I skewed the angle of my lips, gave size
to my young cheeks, inflating them; up rose

one eyebrow, while one went the other way,
and all of this I'd do in seconds flat.
My mum would see, and turn to me to say,
'If the wind changes, your face will stay like that.'

I've just looked in a mirror, and I saw
a face I find it hard to recognise.
It's not the same as what was there before,
a different phizog, much to my surprise,

to what grins out at me in photographs,
which still is twisted in a comic gurn;
the younger me looks at them and he laughs,
the older me is quite intrigued to learn

my mum's advice would have been more accurate
if when a camera came out, she'd said, 'When
the shutter clicks, your face will stay like that
in all these photographs.' If I'd known then

what I know now, I would still make a strange
and silly look appear; for it's the pace
of life and time and how we must face change,
and not the wind, that makes us change our face.

The Darkling Thrush

Thomas Hardy

This Speaker describes the depths of winter but is inspired when they hear a singing thrush.

I leant upon a coppice gate
    When Frost was spectre-grey,
And Winter's dregs made desolate
    The weakening eye of day.
The tangled bine-stems scored the sky
    Like strings of broken lyres,
And all mankind that haunted nigh
    Had sought their household fires.

The land's sharp features seemed to be
    The Century's corpse outleant,
His crypt the cloudy canopy,
    The wind his death-lament.
The ancient pulse of germ and birth
    Was shrunken hard and dry,
And every spirit upon earth
    Seemed fervourless as I.

At once a voice arose among
    The bleak twigs overhead
In a full-hearted evensong
    Of joy illimited;
An aged thrush, frail, gaunt, and small,
    In blast-beruffled plume,
Had chosen thus to fling his soul
    Upon the growing gloom.

So little cause for carolings
    Of such ecstatic sound
Was written on terrestrial things
    Afar or nigh around,
That I could think there trembled through
    His happy good-night air
Some blessed Hope, whereof he knew
    And I was unaware.

Ghareeb

Fatimah Asghar

This poem explores conflicting identities and the struggle to find home.

on visits back your english sticks to everything.
your own auntie calls you ghareeb. stranger

in your family's house, you: runaway dog turned wild.
like your little cousin who pops gum & wears bras now: a stranger.

black grass swaying in the field, glint of gold in her nose.
they say it so often, it must be your name now, stranger.

when'd the west set in your bones? you survive
each winter like you were made for snow, a stranger

to each ancestor who lights your past. your parents,
dead, never taught you their language – stranger

to everything that tries to bring you home. a silver sun
& blood-soaked leaves, everything a little strange

& a little the same – like the hump of a deer on the busy
road, headless, chest propped up as the cars fly by. strange

no one bats an eye. you should pray but you're a bad muslim
everyone says. the Qur'an you memorized turns stranger

in your mouth, sand that quakes your throat. gag & ache
even your body wants nothing to do with you, stranger.

how many poems must you write to convince yourself
you have a family? everyone leaves & you end up the stranger.

'Ghareeb' meaning: stranger, one without a home and thus, deserving of pity.
Also: westerner.

Fairy Song
Louisa May Alcott

This poem describes the environment of a fairy's feast.

The moonlight fades from flower and tree,
And the stars dim one by one;
The tale is told, the song is sung,
And the Fairy feast is done.
The night-wind rocks the sleeping flowers,
And sings to them, soft and low.
The early birds erelong will wake:
'T is time for the Elves to go.

O'er the sleeping earth we silently pass,
Unseen by mortal eye,
And send sweet dreams, as we lightly float
Through the quiet moonlit sky; –
For the stars' soft eyes alone may see,
And the flowers alone may know,
The feasts we hold, the tales we tell;
So 't is time for the Elves to go.

From bird, and blossom, and bee,
We learn the lessons they teach;
And seek, by kindly deeds, to win
A loving friend in each.
And though unseen on earth we dwell,
Sweet voices whisper low,
And gentle hearts most joyously greet
The Elves where'er they go.

When next we meet in the Fairy dell,
May the silver moon's soft light
Shine then on faces gay as now,
And Elfin hearts as light.
Now spread each wing, for the eastern sky
With sunlight soon shall glow.
The morning star shall light us home:
Farewell! for the Elves must go.

On the Discomfort of Being in the Same Room as the Boy You Like

Sarah Kay

This poem contemplates the embarrassment and vulnerability of having a crush on someone.

Everyone is looking at you looking at him.
Everyone can tell. *He can tell.* So you
spend most of your time not looking at him.
The wallpaper, the floor, there are cracks
in the ceiling. Someone has left a can of
iced tea in the corner, it is half-empty,
I mean half-full. There are four light bulbs
in the standing lamp, there is a fan. You
are counting things to keep from looking
at him. Five chairs, two laptops, someone's
umbrella, a hat. People are talking so you
look at their faces. This is a good trick. They
will think you are listening to them and not
thinking about him. Now he is talking. So
you look away. The cracks in the ceiling are
in the shape of a whale or maybe an elephant
with a fat trunk. If he ever falls in love with
you, you will lie on your backs in a field
somewhere and look up at the sky and he will
say, *Baby, look at that silly cloud, it is a whale!*
and you will say, *Baby, that is an elephant
with a fat trunk,* and you will argue for a bit,
but he will love you anyway.

He is asking a question now and no one has
answered it yet. So you lower your eyes from
the plaster and say, *the twenty first, I think,*
and he smiles and says, *oh, cool,* and you
smile back, and you cannot stop your smiling,
oh you cannot stop your smile.

The Queen of Hearts

Christina Rossetti

This poem uses the metaphor of playing cards to explore loss in the game of love.

How comes it, Flora, that, whenever we
Play cards together, you invariably,
  However the pack parts,
  Still hold the Queen of Hearts?

I've scanned you with a scrutinizing gaze,
Resolved to fathom these your secret ways:
  But, sift them as I will,
  Your ways are secret still.

I cut and shuffle; shuffle, cut, again;
But all my cutting, shuffling, proves in vain:
  Vain hope, vain forethought, too;
  That Queen still falls to you.

I dropped her once, prepense; but, ere the deal
Was dealt, your instinct seemed her loss to feel:
  'There should be one card more,'
  You said, and searched the floor.

I cheated once: I made a private notch
In Heart-Queen's back, and kept a lynx-eyed watch;
  Yet such another back
  Deceived me in the pack:

The Queen of Clubs assumed by arts unknown
An imitative dint that seemed my own;
  This notch, not of my doing,
  Misled me to my ruin.

It baffles me to puzzle out the clue,
Which must be skill, or craft, or luck in you:
  Unless, indeed, it be
  Natural affinity.

A Beach On A Foggy Day

Jade Anouka

This poem depicts the beauty and mystery of the world on a foggy day.

There's something truly magical
About looking out from a beach
On a foggy day.

The soft sand sinking beneath your shoes
As the waves kiss
And retract from you
Calling you in
Pushing you away
Calling you in again.

You can't see how far you can see
All you can see is sky
The sky and sea as one
The horizon nowhere.

You look around
You're in a perfect bubble of air
All around is water
You can taste it
The sea or the sky or both.

The mystery of what's beyond
Sings to you
Enticing you into a dream
A day dream
A dream of what's out there
Inside the fog
Beyond the sea

Creatures fly into it
Others fly back
Changed?
They've been where you wish to
The mysterious space
Beyond the fog

Beyond the sea
Where the horizon must be.

That magical place you want to see
So far away
When looking out from a beach
On a foggy day.

Level 3 Speaking Verse and Prose: Grade 6 – Prose

Notes on a Nervous Planet

Matt Haig

This novel examines mental health in the age of technology. In this section, the narrator observes the sky and the stars, contemplating their power and ability to offer hope.

I often wondered, and still wonder, why the sky, especially the night sky, had such an effect. I used to think it was to do with the scale. When you look up at the cosmos you can't help but feel minuscule. You feel the smallness of yourself not only in space but also in time. Because, of course, when you stare into space you are staring up at ancient history. You are staring at stars as they *were*, not as they *are*. Light travels. It doesn't just instantaneously appear. It moves at 186,000 miles per second. Which sounds fast, but also means that light from the closest star to Earth (after the sun) took over four years to get here.

But some of the stars visible to the naked eye are over 15,000 light years away. Which means the light reaching your eye began its journey at the end of the Ice Age. Before humans knew how to farm land. Contrary to popular belief, most of the stars that we see with our eyes are not dead. Stars, unlike us, exist for a very long time. But that adds to, rather than takes away from, the therapeutic majesty of the night sky. Our beautiful but tiny brief role within the cosmos is as that rarest of galactic things: a living, breathing, conscious organism.

When looking at the sky, all our 21st-century worries can be placed in their cosmic context. The sky is bigger than emails and deadlines and mortgages and internet trolls. It is bigger than our minds, and their illnesses. It is bigger than names and nations and dates and clocks. All of our earthly concerns are quite transient when compared to the sky. Through our lives, throughout every chapter of human history, the sky has always been the sky.

And, of course, when we are looking at the sky we aren't looking at something outside ourselves. We are looking, really, at where we came from. As physicist Carl Sagan wrote in his masterpiece *Cosmos*: 'The nitrogen in our DNA, the calcium in our teeth, the iron in our blood, the carbon in our apple pies were made in the interiors of collapsing stars. We are made of starstuff.'

The sky, like the sea, can anchor us. It says: hey, it's okay, there is something bigger than your life that you are part of, and it's – literally – cosmic. It's the most wonderful thing. And you need to make like a tree or a bird and just feel

a part of the great natural order now and again. You are incredible. You are nothing and everything. You are a single moment and all eternity. You are the universe in motion.

Well done.

'The sky is always the sky'

The Mill on the Floss

George Eliot (Mary Ann Evans)

Maggie and Tom Tulliver are siblings growing up at Dorlcote Mill on the River Floss. Mrs Tulliver has instructed Maggie to go upstairs and brush her hair. Feeling rebellious, Maggie decides to instead cut it all off. She involves Tom in her plan, who finds it hilarious, but Maggie soon regrets her impulsive decisions.

'Come upstairs with me, Tom,' she whispered, when they were outside the door. 'There's something I want to do before dinner.'

'There's no time to play at anything before dinner,' said Tom, whose imagination was impatient of any intermediate prospect.

'Oh yes, there is time for this; *do* come, Tom.'

Tom followed Maggie upstairs into her mother's room, and saw her go at once to a drawer, from which she took out a large pair of scissors.

'What are they for, Maggie?' said Tom, feeling his curiosity awakened.

Maggie answered by seizing her front locks and cutting them straight across the middle of her forehead.

'Oh, my buttons! Maggie, you'll catch it!' exclaimed Tom; 'you'd better not cut any more off.'

Snip! went the great scissors again while Tom was speaking, and he couldn't help feeling it was rather good fun; Maggie would look so queer.

'Here, Tom, cut it behind for me,' said Maggie, excited by her own daring, and anxious to finish the deed.

'You'll catch it, you know,' said Tom, nodding his head in an admonitory manner, and hesitating a little as he took the scissors.

'Never mind, make haste!' said Maggie, giving a little stamp with her foot. Her cheeks were quite flushed.

The black locks were so thick, nothing could be more tempting to a lad who had already tasted the forbidden pleasure of cutting the pony's mane. I speak

to those who know the satisfaction of making a pair of scissors meet through a duly resisting mass of hair. One delicious grinding snip, and then another and another, and the hinder-locks fell heavily on the floor, and Maggie stood cropped in a jagged, uneven manner, but with a sense of clearness and freedom, as if she had emerged from a wood into the open plain.

'Oh, Maggie,' said Tom, jumping round her, and slapping his knees as he laughed, 'Oh, my buttons! what a queer thing you look! Look at yourself in the glass; you look like the idiot we throw out nutshells to at school.'

Maggie felt an unexpected pang. She had thought beforehand chiefly at her own deliverance from her teasing hair and teasing remarks about it, and something also of the triumph she should have over her mother and her aunts by this very decided course of action; she didn't want her hair to look pretty, – that was out of the question, – she only wanted people to think her a clever little girl, and not to find fault with her. But now, when Tom began to laugh at her, and say she was like an idiot, the affair had quite a new aspect. She looked in the glass, and still Tom laughed and clapped his hands, and Maggie's cheeks began to pale, and her lips to tremble a little.

Book 1, Chapter 7, 'Enter the Aunts and Uncles'

Boys Don't Cry
Malorie Blackman

Dante Bridgeman is waiting for his A-Level results when his ex-girlfriend shows up with a baby. Dante's baby. She leaves and never returns. Dante's daughter Emma becomes part of the Bridgeman family. On Dante's eighteenth birthday, his brother Adam finds himself in a violent fight with a boy named Josh, which leaves him hospitalised. In this section, Emma sees Adam's injuries for the first time.

My brother went back to his chair and sat down. I watched him for a few moments, my anger fading as I did so. Where was Adam? I longed for my brother to return.

'Adam, how much longer are you going to stay in this room?'

Adam didn't answer. He continued to stare out of his window, his shoulders slumped, his whole attitude one of defeat. I hated seeing him like that. It wasn't my brother sitting in the chair; it was just my brother's shell.

'Daddy?' Emma peeped round the door into Adam's bedroom.

Adam moved round in his chair so that we could no longer see his profile.

'Emma, I left you in the sitting room.' I frowned down at her. I hadn't realized she could make it up the stairs without me. And I only left the child gate closed if Emma was already upstairs.

'Heyo, Unckey...' Emma's version of 'Hello, Uncle' greeted Adam, the uncertainty in her voice very evident. She hadn't seen Adam properly in weeks and could still probably remember him shouting at her.

'Dante, could you leave, please?' said Adam, turning round further in his chair so we had a good view of the back of his head.

Emma toddled into the bedroom before I could stop her. 'Heyo, Unckey,' she said again. 'Heyo.'

Adam stiffened in his chair at the sound of her voice getting closer. He desperately wanted me to take Emma and leave, but something held me back.

Emma waddled around the chair to face Adam. She looked up at him, then smiled, her arms outstretched.

Adam looked down at his niece.

Emma wriggled her arms at Adam, her meaning clear. Slowly Adam bent to pick her up. I released the air in my lungs with a hiss. I hadn't even realized that I was holding my breath. Adam placed Emma on his lap. I moved further into the room. My brother was holding Emma like she might break. I realized with a start that he was giving her a chance to bolt, to run and hide from his face. Emma reached out one small hand and stroked the scars on Adam's cheek.

'Hurts?' she asked.

'Yes,' Adam whispered.

'Lots?'

'Lots.'

'Kiss?'

Adam sighed, then smiled – the first real smile I'd seen from him in a long, long time. 'Yes, please.'

Emma clambered to stand on Adam's thigh whilst he still held her. She leaned forward and kissed his scar-ridden cheek, then she wrapped both arms around his neck and held him as tightly as he held her.

And I could see from where I was standing that Adam was crying.

Chapter 44, 'Dante'

The Strange Case of Dr Jekyll and Mr Hyde

Robert Louis Stevenson

Following a series of murders from the mysterious criminal Mr Hyde, Gabriel John Utterson (a lawyer and close friend of Dr Jekyll) seeks to investigate the identity of Hyde. It is revealed that Dr Jekyll and Mr Hyde are the same person, where Dr Jekyll transforms into Mr Hyde upon drinking a serum. However, in this section, Dr Jekyll involuntarily transforms into Mr Hyde whilst sleeping.

It was in vain I looked about me; in vain I saw the decent furniture and tall proportions of my room in the square; in vain that I recognised the pattern of the bed curtains and the design of the mahogany frame; something still kept insisting that I was not where I was, that I had not wakened where I seemed to be, but in the little room in Soho where I was accustomed to sleep in the body of Edward Hyde. I smiled to myself, and, in my psychological way, began lazily to inquire into the elements of this illusion, occasionally, even as I did so, dropping back into a comfortable morning doze. I was still so engaged when, in one of my more wakeful moments, my eye fell upon my hand. Now, the hand of Henry Jekyll (as you have often remarked) was professional in shape and size; it was large, firm, white and comely. But the hand which I now saw, clearly enough in the yellow light of a mid-London morning, lying half shut on the bedclothes, was lean, corded, knuckly, of a dusky pallor, and thickly shaded with a swart growth of hair. It was the hand of Edward Hyde.

I must have stared upon it for near half a minute, sunk as I was in the mere stupidity of wonder, before terror woke up in my breast as sudden and startling as the crash of cymbals; and bounding from my bed I rushed to the mirror. At the sight that met my eyes, my blood was changed into something exquisitely thin and icy. Yes, I had gone to bed Henry Jekyll, I had awakened Edward Hyde. How was this to be explained? I asked myself; and then, with another bound of terror – how was it to be remedied? It was well on in the morning; the servants were up; all my drugs were in the cabinet – a long journey down two pairs of stairs, through the back passage, across the open court and through the anatomical theatre, from where I was then standing horror-struck. It might indeed be possible to cover my face; but of what use was that, when I was unable to conceal the alteration in my stature? And then with an overpowering sweetness of relief, it came back upon my mind that the servants were already used to the coming and going of my second self. I had soon dressed, as well as I was able, in clothes of my own size: had soon passed through the house, where Bradshaw stared and drew back at seeing Mr Hyde at such an hour and in such a strange array; and ten minutes later, Dr Jekyll had returned to

his own shape, and was sitting down, with a darkened brow, to make a feint of breakfasting.

Small indeed was my appetite.

'Henry Jekyll's Full Statement of the Case'

Conversations with Friends

Sally Rooney

Frances and Bobbi are best friends and ex-girlfriends. As they become involved with a couple named Nick and Melissa, Frances and Nick start an affair. Before this section, Bobbi and Frances have been staying with the couple in France, where Bobbi finds out the truth about the affair.

It was late August. In the airport Bobbi asked me: how long has that been going on for, between the two of you? And I told her. She shrugged like, okay. On the bus back from Dublin airport, we heard a news report about a woman who had died in hospital. It was a case I had been following some time ago and forgotten about. We were too tired to talk about it then anyway. It was raining against the bus windows as we pulled up outside college. I helped Bobbi lift her suitcase out of the luggage compartment and she rolled down the sleeves of her raincoat. Lashing, she said. Typical. I was getting the train back to Ballina to stay with my mother for a few nights, and I told Bobbi I would call her. She flagged a taxi and I walked towards the bus stop to get the 145 to Heuston.

When I arrived in Ballina that night, my mother put on a bolognese and I sat at the kitchen table teasing the knots out of my hair. Outside the kitchen window the leaves dripped rain like squares of watered silk. She said I was tanned. I let a few slip hairs fall form my fingers to the kitchen floor and said: oh, am I? I knew I was.

Did you hear from your father at all while you were over there? she said.

He called me once. He didn't know where I was, he sounded drunk.

She took a plastic packet of garlic bread from the fridge. My throat hurt and I couldn't think of what to say.

He wasn't always this bad, right? I said. It's gotten worse.

He's your father, Frances. You tell me.

I don't exactly hang out with him on the day-to-day.

The kettle came to boil, releasing a cloud of steam over the hob and toaster. I shivered. I couldn't believe I had woken up in France that morning.

I mean, was he like this when you married him? I said.

She didn't reply. I looked out at the garden, at the bird-feeder hanging off the birch tree. My mother favoured some species of birds over others; the feeder was for the benefit of small and appealingly vulnerable ones. Crows were completely out of favour. She chased them away when she spotted them. They're all just birds, I pointed out. She said yes, but some birds can fend for themselves.

I could feel a headache coming on while I set the table, though I didn't want to mention it. Whenever I told my mother I had headaches she always said it was because I didn't eat enough and I had low blood sugar, although I had never looked up the science behind that claim. By the time the food was ready I could feel a pain in my back too, like a kind of nerve or muscular pain that made sitting straight uncomfortable.

Part 2, Chapter 18

Jane Eyre
Charlotte Brontë

Jane Eyre is in love with Rochester, but their relationship is tinged with secrets. After having agreed to marry him, Jane discovers that Rochester is married to a woman named Bertha, who he hides on the third floor of Thornfield Manor. In this section, Jane flees.

Drearily I wound my way downstairs: I knew what I had to do, and I did it mechanically. I sought the key of the side-door in the kitchen; I sought, too, a phial of oil and a feather; I oiled the key and the lock. I got some water, I got some bread: for perhaps I should have to walk far; and my strength, sorely shaken of late, must not break down. All this I did without one sound. I opened the door, passed out, shut it softly. Dim dawn glimmered in the yard. The great gates were closed and locked; but a wicket in one of them was only latched. Through that I departed: it, too, I shut; and now I was out of Thornfield.

A mile off, beyond the fields, lay a road which stretched in the contrary direction to Millcote; a road I had never travelled, but often noticed, and wondered where it led: thither I bent my steps. No reflection was to be allowed now: not one glance was to be cast back; not even one forward. Not one thought was to be given either to the past or the future. The first was a page so heavenly sweet – so deadly sad – that to read one line of it would dissolve my courage and break down my energy. The last was an awful blank: something like the world when the deluge was gone by.

I skirted fields, and hedges, and lanes till after sunrise. I believe it was a lovely summer morning: I know my shoes, which I had put on when I left the house, were soon wet with dew.

But I looked neither to rising sun, nor smiling sky, nor wakening nature. He who is taken out to pass through a fair scene to the scaffold, thinks not of the flowers that smile on his road, but of the block and axe-edge; of the disseverment of bone and vein; of the grave gaping at the end: and I thought of drear flight and homeless wandering – and oh! with agony I thought of what I left. I could not help it. I thought of him now – in his room – watching the sunrise; hoping I should soon come to say I would stay with him and be his. I longed to be his; I panted to return: it was not too late; I could yet spare him the bitter pang of bereavement. As yet my flight, I was sure, was undiscovered. I could go back and be his comforter – his pride; his redeemer from misery, perhaps from

ruin. Oh, that fear of his self-abandonment – far worse than my abandonment – how it goaded me! It was a barbed arrow-head in my breast; it tore me when I tried to extract it; it sickened me when remembrance thrust it farther in. Birds began singing in brake and copse: birds were faithful to their mates; birds were emblems of love. What was I?

Chapter 27

The Hate U Give

Angie Thomas

When Starr witnesses the fatal shooting of her childhood best friend Khalil at the hands of a police officer, Khalil's death hits the news and Starr takes on a public role. Starr gives news interviews and speaks at protests. This section depicts the protest that follows the grand jury's decision not to charge the police officer for Khalil's murder.

A voice in the distance says something, I can't make it out, and there's a thunderous response like from a crowd.

Chris and I walk behind the other two. His hand falls to his side, and he brushes up against me, his sly way of trying to hold my hand. I let him.

A Rottweiler on a leash in a fenced-in yard barks and struggles to come after us. I stomp my foot at it. It squeals and jumps back.

'She's all right,' Seven says, though it seems like he's trying to convince himself. 'Yeah. She's fine.'

A block away, people stand around in a four-way intersection, watching something on one of the other streets.

'You need to exit the street,' a voice announces from a loudspeaker. 'You are unlawfully blocking traffic.'

'A hairbrush is not a gun! A hairbrush is not a gun!' a voice chants from another loudspeaker. It's echoed back by a crowd.

We get to the intersection. A red, green, and yellow school bus is parked on the street to our right. It says Just Us for Justice on the side. A large crowd is gathered in the street to our left. They point black hairbrushes into the air.

The protestors are on Carnation. Where it happened.

I haven't been back here since that night. Knowing this is where Khalil... I stare too hard, the crowd disappears, and I see him lying in the street. The whole thing plays out before my eyes like a horror movie on repeat. He looks at me for the last time and –

'A hairbrush is not a gun!'

The voice snaps me from my daze.

Ahead of the crowd a lady with twists stands on top of a police car, holding a bullhorn. She turns towards us, her fist raised for black power. Khalil smiles on the front of her T-shirt.

'Ain't that your attorney, Starr?' Seven asks.

'Yeah.' Now I knew Ms. Ofrah was about that radical life, but when you think 'attorney' you don't really think 'person standing on a police car with a bullhorn,' you know?

'Disperse immediately,' the officer repeats. I can't see him for the crowd.

Ms Ofrah leads the chant again. 'A hairbrush is not a gun! A hairbrush is not a gun!'

It's contagious and echoes all around us. Seven, DeVante, and Chris join in.

'A hairbrush is not a gun,' I mutter.

Khalil drops it into the side of the door.

'A hairbrush is not a gun.'

He opens the door to ask if I'm okay.

Then pow-pow –

'A hairbrush is not a gun!' I scream as loud as I can, fist high in the air, tears in my eyes.

Chapter 24

The Time Machine

H. G. Wells

A Time Traveller has a theory that time is the fourth dimension. Using a time machine, the Time Traveller starts to test this theory, and this section explores the sensation of time travel.

I took the starting lever in one hand and the stopping one in the other, pressed the first, and almost immediately the second. I seemed to reel; I felt a nightmare sensation of falling; and, looking round, I saw the laboratory exactly as before. Had anything happened? For a moment I suspected that my intellect had tricked me. Then I noted the clock. A moment before, as it seemed, it had stood at a minute or so past ten; now it was nearly half-past three!

I drew a breath, set my teeth, gripped the starting lever with both hands, and went off with a thud. The laboratory got hazy and went dark. Mrs Watchett came in and walked, apparently without seeing me, towards the garden door. I suppose it took her a minute or so to traverse the place, but to me she seemed to shoot across the room like a rocket. I pressed the lever over to its extreme position. The night came like the turning out of a lamp, and in another moment came tomorrow. The laboratory grew faint and hazy, then fainter and ever fainter. Tomorrow night came black, then day again, night again, day again, faster and faster still. An eddying murmur filled my ears, and a strange, dumb confusedness descended on my mind.

I am afraid I cannot convey the peculiar sensations of time travelling. They are excessively unpleasant. There is a feeling exactly like that one has upon a switchback – of a helpless headlong motion! I felt the same horrible anticipation, too, of an imminent smash. As I put on pace, night followed day like the flapping of a black wing. The dim suggestion of the laboratory seemed presently to fall away from me, and I saw the sun hopping swiftly across the sky, leaping it every minute, and every minute marking a day. I supposed the laboratory had been destroyed and I had come into the open air. I had a dim impression of scaffolding, but I was already going too fast to be conscious of any moving things. The slowest snail that ever crawled dashed by too fast for me. The twinkling succession of darkness and light was excessively painful to the eye. Then, in the intermittent darknesses, I saw the moon spinning swiftly through her quarters from new to full, and had a faint glimpse of the circling stars. Presently, as I went on, still gaining velocity, the palpitation of night and day merged into one continuous greyness; the sky took on a wonderful deepness of blue, a splendid luminous colour like that of early twilight; the

jerking sun became a streak of fire, a brilliant arch, in space; the moon a fainter fluctuating band; and I could see nothing of the stars, save now and then a brighter circle flickering in the blue.

Chapter 4, 'Time Travelling'

Level 3 Speaking Verse and Prose: Grade 7 – Verse

I Hope You Stopped for the Swans

Cecilia Knapp

This poem explores the impact of a son's death on his father and family.

It's hard to recognise longing
filling up the body like a rock pool.
Looking behind me at the wall.
Why is it always four o'clock?

I hear knocking when I'm sleeping,
but don't see your face anymore.
Come inside. Shake the water off, my love,
you've had a skinful.

Somewhere our dad is on a hill
with his waterproof map.
He'll send me a long text later about
being at London Bridge, eating a Cornish pasty.

I'll reply, 'Renationalise the railways!'
by which I mean, I love you
and I'm sorry your son died.
How we used to beg him to bury us in the sand.

There are small mercies; my soft father.
I don't think about him crumbling apart
on the kitchen stool,
how seven minutes later he was back to normal,
singing under his breath, spreading apricot jam.
The sky is thin today
like a torn-off blister
and he is underneath it, walking.

The Second Coming

William Butler Yeats

This apocalyptic poem describes a world overrun by chaos.

Turning and turning in the widening gyre
The falcon cannot hear the falconer;
Things fall apart; the centre cannot hold;
Mere anarchy is loosed upon the world,
The blood-dimmed tide is loosed, and everywhere
The ceremony of innocence is drowned;
The best lack all conviction, while the worst
Are full of passionate intensity.

Surely some revelation is at hand;
Surely the Second Coming is at hand.
The Second Coming! Hardly are those words out
When a vast image out of *Spiritus Mundi*
Troubles my sight: a waste of desert sand;
A shape with lion body and the head of a man,
A gaze blank and pitiless as the sun,
Is moving its slow thighs, while all about it
Wind shadows of the indignant desert birds.
The darkness drops again but now I know
That twenty centuries of stony sleep
Were vexed to nightmare by a rocking cradle,
And what rough beast, its hour come round at last,
Slouches towards Bethlehem to be born?

What You Mourn

Sheila Black

Exploring disability, this poem questions society's labels and assumptions.

The year they straightened my legs,
the young doctor said, meaning to be kind,
Now you will walk straight
on your wedding day, but what he could not
imagine is how even on my wedding day
I would arch back and wonder
about that body I had before I was changed,
how I would have nested in it,
made it my home, how I repeated his words
when I wished to stir up my native anger
feel like the exile I believed
I was, imprisoned in a foreign body
like a person imprisoned in a foreign land
forced to speak a strange tongue
heavy in the mouth, a mouth full of stones.

Crippled they called us when I was young
later the word was *disabled* and then *differently abled,*
but those were all names given by outsiders,
none of whom could imagine
that the crooked body they spoke of,
the body, which made walking difficult
and running practically impossible,
except as a kind of dance, a sideways looping
like someone about to fall
headlong down and hug the earth, that body
they tried so hard to fix, straighten was simply mine,
and I loved it as you love your own country
the familiar lay of the land, the unkempt trees,
the smell of mowed grass, down to the nameless
flowers at your feet – clover, asphodel,
and the blue flies that buzz over them.

From **The Rime of the Ancient Mariner**
Samuel Taylor Coleridge

This poem recounts the experience of a sailor who shot an albatross whilst on board a ship.

The ice was here, the ice was there,
The ice was all around:
It cracked and growled, and roared and howled,
Like noises in a swound!

At length did cross an Albatross:
Thorough the fog it came;
As if it had been a Christian soul,
We hailed it in God's name.

It ate the food it ne'er had eat,
And round and round it flew.
The ice did split with a thunder-fit;
The helmsman steered us through!

And a good south wind sprung up behind;
The Albatross did follow,
And every day, for food or play,
Came to the mariners' hollo!

In mist or cloud, on mast or shroud,
It perched for vespers nine;
Whiles all the night, through fog-smoke white,
Glimmered the white Moon-shine.

'God save thee, ancient Mariner!
From the fiends, that plague thee thus! –
Why look'st thou so?' – With my cross-bow
I shot the ALBATROSS.

Because I could not stop for Death

Emily Dickinson

This poem explores the inevitability of death, which is personified as a carriage-driver.

Because I could not stop for Death –
He kindly stopped for me –
The Carriage held but just Ourselves –
And Immortality.

We slowly drove – He knew no haste
And I had put away
My labor and my leisure too,
For His Civility –

We passed the School, where Children strove
At Recess – in the Ring –
We passed the Fields of Gazing Grain –
We passed the Setting Sun –

Or rather – He passed us –
The Dews drew quivering and chill –
For only Gossamer, my Gown –
My Tippet – only Tulle –

We paused before a House that seemed
A Swelling of the Ground –
The Roof was scarcely visible –
The Cornice – in the Ground –

Since then – 'tis Centuries – and yet
Feels shorter than the Day
I first surmised the Horses' Heads
Were toward Eternity –

Another Planet

Dunya Mikhail, translated by **Kareem James Abu-Zeid**

This poem presents the possibility of leaving Earth for another planet.

I have a special ticket
to another planet
beyond this Earth.
A comfortable world, and beautiful:
a world without much smoke,
not too hot
and not too cold.
The creatures
are gentler there,
and the governments
have no secrets.
The police are nonexistent:
there are no problems
and no fights.
And the schools
don't exhaust their students
with too much work
for history has yet to start
and there's no geography
and no other languages.
And even better:
the war
has left its 'r' behind
and turned into love,
so the weapons sleep
beneath the dust,
and the planes pass by
without shelling the cities,
and the boats
look like smiles
on the water.
All things
are peaceful
and kind
on the other planet
beyond this Earth.
But still I hesitate
to go alone.

The Other Side of a Mirror

Mary Elizabeth Coleridge

This poem explores femininity, gender stereotypes and dissociation.

I sat before my glass one day,
And conjured up a vision bare,
Unlike the aspects glad and gay,
That erst were found reflected there –
The vision of a woman, wild
With more than womanly despair.

Her hair stood back on either side
A face bereft of loveliness.
It had no envy now to hide
What once no man on earth could guess.
It formed the thorny aureole
Of hard unsanctified distress.

Her lips were open – not a sound
Came through the parted lines of red.
Whate'er it was, the hideous wound
In silence and in secret bled.
No sigh relieved her speechless woe,
She had no voice to speak her dread.

And in her lurid eyes there shone
The dying flame of life's desire,
Made mad because its hope was gone,
And kindled at the leaping fire
Of jealousy, and fierce revenge,
And strength that could not change nor tire.

Shade of a shadow in the glass,
O set the crystal surface free!
Pass – as the fairer visions pass –
Nor ever more return, to be
The ghost of a distracted hour,
That heard me whisper, 'I am she!'

Life Doesn't Frighten Me

Maya Angelou

This poem celebrates courage and bravery.

Shadows on the wall
Noises down the hall
Life doesn't frighten me at all
Bad dogs barking loud
Big ghosts in a cloud
Life doesn't frighten me at all

Mean old Mother Goose
Lions on the loose
They don't frighten me at all
Dragons breathing flame
On my counterpane
That doesn't frighten me at all.

I go boo
Make them shoo
I make fun
Way they run
I won't cry
So they fly
I just smile
They go wild
Life doesn't frighten me at all.

Tough guys in a fight
All alone at night
Life doesn't frighten me at all.
Panthers in the park
Strangers in the dark
No, they don't frighten me at all.

That new classroom where
Boys all pull my hair
(Kissy little girls
With their hair in curls)
They don't frighten me at all.

Don't show me frogs and snakes
And listen for my scream,
If I'm afraid at all
It's only in my dreams.

I've got a magic charm
That I keep up my sleeve
I can walk the ocean floor
And never have to breathe.

Life doesn't frighten me at all
Not at all
Not at all.
Life doesn't frighten me at all.

Level 3 Speaking Verse and Prose: Grade 7 – Prose

Educated

Tara Westover

Tara Westover grew up in a Mormon family where she is not allowed to go to school, get a birth certificate or attend a medical appointment. As she grows up, Tara becomes curious about enlarging her world and applies to Brigham Young University (BYU). This section explores Tara's conflicting feelings towards her education.

This caused a kind of crisis in me. My love of music, and my desire to study it, had been compatible with my idea of what a woman is. My love of history and politics and world affairs was not. And yet they called to me.

A few days before finals, I sat for an hour with my friend Josh in an empty classroom. He was reviewing his applications for law school. I was choosing my courses for the next semester.

'If you were a woman,' I asked, 'would you still study law?'

Josh didn't look up. 'If I were a woman,' he said, 'I wouldn't *want* to study it.'

'But you've talked about nothing except law school for as long as I've known you,' I said. 'It's your dream, isn't it?'

'It is,' he admitted. 'But it wouldn't be if I were a woman. Women are made differently. They don't have this ambition. Their ambition is for children.' He smiled at me as if I knew what he was talking about. And I did. I smiled, and for a few seconds we were in agreement.

Then: 'But what if you were a woman, and somehow you felt exactly as you do now?'

Josh's eyes fixed on the wall for a moment. He was really thinking about it. Then he said, 'I'd know something was wrong with me.'

I'd been wondering whether something was wrong with me since the beginning of the semester, when I'd attended my first lecture on world affairs. I'd been wondering how I could be a woman and yet be drawn to unwomanly things.

I knew someone must have the answer so I decided to ask one of my professors. I chose the professor of my Jewish history class, because he was

quiet and soft-spoken. Dr. Kerry was a short man with dark eyes and a serious expression. He lectured in a thick wool jacket even in hot weather. I knocked on his office door quietly, as if I hoped he wouldn't answer, and soon was sitting silently across from him. I didn't know what my question was, and Dr. Kerry didn't ask. Instead he posed general questions – about my grades, what courses I was taking. He asked why I'd chosen Jewish history, and without thinking I blurted that I'd learned of the Holocaust only a few semesters before and wanted to learn the rest of the story.

'You learned of the Holocaust when?' he said.

'At BYU.'

'They didn't teach about it in your school?'

'They probably did,' I said. 'Only I wasn't there.'

'Where were you?'

I explained as best I could, that my parents didn't believe in public education, that they'd kept us at home. When I'd finished, he laced his fingers as if contemplating a difficult problem. 'I think you should stretch yourself. See what happens.'

Chapter 27, 'If I Were a Woman'

The Portrait of a Lady

Henry James

Isabel Archer is an American woman living in Europe. Isabel has married Gilbert Osmond, an American expatriate. After having settled in Rome, their marriage begins to deteriorate due to intellectual differences and contrasting world views. This section provides an insight into Isabel's mind.

She had too many ideas for herself; but that was just what one married for, to share them with someone else. One couldn't pluck them up by the roots, though of course one might suppress them, be careful not to utter them. It had not been this, however, his objecting to her opinions; this had been nothing. She had no opinions – none that she would not have been eager to sacrifice in the satisfaction of feeling herself loved for it. What he had meant had been the whole thing – her character, the way she felt, the way she judged. This was what she had kept in reserve; this was what he had not known until he had found himself – with the door closed behind, as it were – set down face to face with it. She had a certain way of looking at life which he took as a personal offence. Heaven knew that now at least it was a very humble, accommodating way! The strange thing was that she should not have suspected from the first that his own had been so different. She had thought it so large, so enlightened, so perfectly that of an honest man and a gentleman. Hadn't he assured her that he had no superstitions, no dull limitations, no prejudices that had lost their freshness? Hadn't he all the appearance of a man living in the open air of the world, indifferent to small considerations, caring only for truth and knowledge and believing that two intelligent people ought to look for them together and, whether they found them or not, find at least some happiness in the search? He had told her he loved the conventional; but there was a sense in which this seemed a noble declaration. In that sense, that of the love of harmony and order and decency and of all the stately offices of life, she went with him freely, and his warning had contained nothing ominous. But when, as the months had elapsed, she had followed him further and he had led her into the mansion of his own habitation, then, then she had seen where she really was.

She could live it over again, the incredulous terror with which she had taken the measure of her dwelling. Between those four walls she had lived ever since; they were to surround her for the rest of her life. It was the house of darkness, the house of dumbness, the house of suffocation. Osmond's beautiful mind gave it neither light nor air; Osmond's beautiful mind indeed seemed to peep down from a small high window and mock at her. Of course it had not been physical suffering; for physical suffering there might have been a remedy. She

could come and go; she had her liberty; her husband was perfectly polite. He took himself so seriously; it was something appalling. Under all his culture, his cleverness, his amenity, under his good-nature, his facility, his knowledge of life, his egotism lay hidden like a serpent in a bank of flowers.

Chapter 42

The Lonely Londoners
Sam Selvon

Set in London in the 1950s, the Tolroy family arrive in London from the West Indies, with the intention of establishing a new life. This passage explores the poverty, oppression and challenges of surviving in London.

The place where Tolroy and the family living was off the Harrow Road, and the people in that area call the Working Class. Wherever in London that it have Working Class, there you will find a lot of spades. This is the real world, where men know what it is to hustle a pound to pay the rent when Friday come. The houses around here old and grey and weatherbeaten, the walls cracking like the last days of Pompeii, it ain't have no hot water, and in the whole street that Tolroy and them living in, none of the houses have bath. You had was to buy one of them big galvanise basin and boil the water and full it up, or else go to the public bath. Some of the houses still had gas light, which is to tell you how old they was. All the houses in a row in the street, on both sides, they build like one long house with walls separating them in parts, so your house jam-up between two neighbours: is so most of the houses is in London. The street does be always dirty except if rain fall. Sometimes a truck does come with a kind of revolving broom and some pipes letting out water, and the driver drive near the pavement, and water come out of the pipes and the broom revolve, and so they sweep the road. It always have little children playing in the road, because they ain't have no other place to play. They does draw hopscotch blocks on the pavement, and other things, and some of the walls of the buildings have signs painted like Vote Labour and Down With the Tories. The bottom of the street, it had a sweet-shop, a bakery, a grocery, a butcher and a fish and chips. The top of the street, where it join the Harrow Road, it had all kind of thing – shop, store, butcher, greengrocer, trolley and bus stop. Up here on a Saturday plenty vendors used to be selling provisions near the pavements. It had a truck used to come one time with flowers to sell, and the fellars used to sell cheap, and the poor people buy tulip and daffodil to put in the dingy room they living in.

It have people living in London who don't know what happening in the room next to them, far more the street, or how other people living. London is a place like that. It divide up in little worlds, and you stay in the world you belong to and you don't know anything about what happening in the other ones except what you read in the papers. Them rich people who does live in Belgravia and Knightsbridge and up in Hampstead and them other plush places, they would never believe what it like in a grim place like Harrow Road or Notting Hill.

Dracula
Bram Stoker

After Count Dracula moves to Whitby in England, a group led by Abraham Van Helsing set out to hunt and kill him. Lucy Westenra becomes ill after visiting Whitby with her friend Mina Murray. Shortly after she dies, Helsing and his companions visit her tomb and discover that she is a vampire. This section depicts their first sighting of Lucy as a vampire.

In respectful silence we took the places assigned to us close round the tomb, but hidden from the sight of any one approaching. I pitied the others, especially Arthur. I had myself been apprenticed by my former visits to this watching horror; and yet I, who had up to an hour ago repudiated the proofs, felt my heart sink within me. Never did tombs look so ghastly white; never did cypress, or yew, or juniper so seem the embodiment of funereal gloom; never did tree or grass wave or rustle so ominously; never did bough creak so mysteriously; and never did the far-away howling of dogs send such a woeful presage through the night.

There was a long spell of silence, a big, aching void, and then from the Professor a keen 'S-s-s-s!' He pointed; and far down the avenue of yews we saw a white figure advance – a dim white figure, which held something dark at its breast. The figure stopped, and at the moment a ray of moonlight fell upon the masses of driving clouds and showed in startling prominence a dark-haired woman, dressed in the cerements of the grave. We could not see the face, for it was bent down over what we saw to be a fair-haired child. There was a pause and a sharp little cry, such as a child gives in sleep, or a dog as it lies before the fire and dreams. We were starting forward, but the Professor's warning hand, seen by us as he stood behind a yew-tree, kept us back; and then as we looked the white figure moved forwards again. It was now near enough for us to see clearly, and the moonlight still held. My own heart grew cold as ice, and I could hear the gasp of Arthur, as we recognised the features of Lucy Westenra. Lucy Westenra, but yet how changed. The sweetness was turned to adamantine, heartless cruelty, and the purity to voluptuous wantonness. Van Helsing stepped out, and, obedient to his gesture, we all advanced too; the four of us ranged in a line before the door of the tomb. Van Helsing raised his lantern and drew the slide; by the concentrated light that fell on Lucy's face we could see that the lips were crimson with fresh blood, and that the stream had trickled over her chin and stained the purity of her lawn death-robe.

We shuddered with horror. I could see by the tremulous light that even Van Helsing's iron nerve had failed. Arthur was next to me, and if I had not seized his arm and held him up, he would have fallen.

When Lucy – I call the thing that was before us Lucy because it bore her shape – saw us she drew back with an angry snarl, such as a cat gives when taken unawares; then her eyes ranged over us. Lucy's eyes in form and colour; but Lucy's eyes unclean and full of hell-fire, instead of the pure, gentle orbs we knew.

Chapter 16, 'Dr Seward's Diary – continued'

Home Fire

Kamila Shamsie

*Set amongst the British Muslim community, Aneeka and Parvaiz are twins who
have been brought up by their older sister Isma. Parvaiz decides to join ISIS
in Syria, but soon realises his mistake and attempts to come home to Britain.
During Parvaiz's attempts to escape ISIS, he is shot. In this section, Aneeka
learns that her twin sibling is dead.*

It was not a possibility her mind knew how to contain. Everyone else in the
world, yes. Everyone else in the world, inescapably. Some in stages: their
grandfather, for weeks half paralysed, unable to speak, even his breath
unfamiliar. Some in a thunderclap: their mother, dropping dead on the floor of
the travel agency where she worked, leaving behind the morning's teacup with
her lipstick on the rim, treasured until the day one of her twins stood up in a
rage and swung the cup by its handle, smashing their mother's mouth. (Aneeka
was sure she had done it; Parvaiz insisted it was him). Some in sleight of hand:
their grandmother, waiting for the test results that they had already decided
would be presented as a death sentence, crossing the road as a drunk driver
took a turn too fast; the doctor called two weeks later with the good news
that the tumour was benign. Some as abstraction: their father, never a living
presence in their life, dead for years before they knew to attach that word
to him. Everyone died, everyone but the twins who looked at each other to
understand their own grief.

Grief manifested itself in ways that felt like anything but grief; grief obliterated
all feelings but grief; grief made a twin wear the same shirt for days on end to
preserve the morning on which the dead were still living; grief made a twin peel
stars off the ceiling and lie in bed with glowing points adhered to fingertips;
grief was bad-tempered, grief was kind; grief saw nothing but itself, grief saw
every speck of pain in the world; grief spread its wings like an eagle, grief
huddled small like a porcupine; grief needed company, grief craved solitude;
grief wanted to remember, wanted to forget; grief raged, grief whimpered; grief
made time compress and contract; grief tasted like hunger, felt like numbness,
sounded like silence; grief tasted like bile, felt like blades, sounded like all the
noise of the world. Grief was a shapeshifter, and invisible too; grief could be
captured as a reflection in a twin's eye. Grief heard its death sentence the
morning you both woke up and one was singing and the other caught the song.

When she received the words that made her singular for the first time in her
life, she pushed them away. It was not true, they meant someone else, it wasn't

him. Where was the proof, bring him to me. No, they couldn't do these things because it was not him. If it had been him it wouldn't be this man sitting in Aunty Naseem's living room bringing the news, a plastic comb sticking out of his breast pocket. He wasn't one of yours, she told the man; we aren't yours.

Chapter 7, 'Aneeka'

Sense and Sensibility
Jane Austen

Marianne and Elinor are sisters. Elinor is romantically attached to Edward Ferrars. However, it is revealed that Edward is secretly engaged to someone else, a woman named Lucy Steele. In this section, Elinor speaks to her sister Marianne about the engagement.

'Edward will marry Lucy; he will marry a woman superior in person and understanding to half her sex; and time and habit will teach him to forget that he ever thought another superior to her.'

'If such is your way of thinking,' said Marianne, 'if the loss of what is most valued is so easily to be made up by something else, your resolution, your self-command, are, perhaps, a little less to be wondered at. – They are brought more within my comprehension.'

'I understand you. You do not suppose that I have ever felt much. For four months, Marianne, I have had all this hanging on my mind, without being at liberty to speak of it to a single creature; knowing that it would make you and my mother most unhappy whenever it were explained to you, yet unable to prepare you for it in the least. It was told me, – it was in a manner forced on me by the very person herself, whose prior engagement ruined all my prospects; and told me, as I thought, with triumph. This person's suspicions, therefore, I have had to oppose, by endeavouring to appear indifferent where I have been most deeply interested; and it has not been only once; I have had her hopes and exultation to listen to again and again. I have known myself to be divided from Edward for ever, without hearing one circumstance that could make me less desire the connection. Nothing has proved him unworthy; nor has anything declared him indifferent to me. I have had to contend against the unkindness of his sister, and the insolence of his mother; and have suffered the punishment of an attachment, without enjoying its advantages. And all this has been going on at a time, when, as you know too well, it has not been my only unhappiness. If you can think me capable of ever feeling, surely you may suppose that I have suffered *now*. The composure of mind with which I have brought myself at present to consider the matter, the consolation that I have been willing to admit, have been the effect of constant and painful exertion; they did not spring up of themselves; they did not occur to relieve my spirits at first. No, Marianne. *Then*, if I had not been bound to silence, perhaps nothing could have kept me entirely – not even what I owed to my dearest friends – from openly showing that I was *very* unhappy.'

Marianne was quite subdued.

'Oh! Elinor,' she cried, 'you have made me hate myself for ever. – How barbarous have I been to you! – you, who have been my only comfort, who have borne with me in all my misery, who have seemed to be only suffering for me! – Is this my gratitude? – Is this the only return I can make you? – Because your merit cries out upon myself, I have been trying to do it away.'

The tenderest caresses followed this confession.

Chapter 37

Black and British: A short, essential history
David Olusoga

This book is an introduction to Black British history. It spans the diverse society of Roman times, foregrounds the Black soldiers who fought during the First World War, and discusses more modern history such as the Windrush Generation. This section covers the Windrush Scandal.

The *Windrush*, the ship that has become the symbol of post-war migration and multicultural Britain, has become a part of the British national story, part of the vocabulary of the nation. There is a Windrush Square in Brixton, a heritage plaque in Tilbury marks the spot where the ship docked and the West Indian migrants came ashore, and a musical based on the lives and ambitions of the *Windrush* migrants enjoyed a successful run in London's West End. Since 2018, the seventieth anniversary of the arrival of the *Windrush*, 22 June has been designated Windrush Day. Yet despite all this, six years after the *Windrush* was celebrated in the opening ceremony at the London Olympic Games, the Guardian newspaper uncovered what become known as the Windrush Scandal.

Under what was called the 'hostile environment', thousands of British people of West Indian heritage, most of whom had come to Britain, often as children, in the 1960s and 1970s, had been stripped of their British citizenship. Many had lost their jobs, and when unable to pay their rent or mortgage, some had lost their homes. Others had been denied the medical treatment in the same National Health Service hospitals that their parents' generation had worked in. Some had even been placed in detention centres or even deported back to countries they had not set foot in since they were children and in which they had no friends or family. Those deported were not allowed to return to the UK.

The victims of the Windrush Scandal were people who had been given the automatic right to remain in the UK on arrival in the 1960s and early 1970s, but to whom no documents were ever issued to prove their status as British citizens. After living in Britain for decades and having worked and paid their taxes throughout their lives, they were suddenly stripped of their British citizenship. The Home Office had been warned years earlier that immigration policy was affected older people from the West Indies but those warnings were ignored. When the scandal was revealed, the Black MP David Lammy, himself the son of Black migrants from Guyana, described the Windrush Scandal as a 'national day of shame'.

Two years later, in 2020, following the murder of George Floyd, an African-American man, a series of Black Lives Matter protests spread across the world. Thousands of people in Britain, most of them young, many of them still at school, organised protests and marched against racism. In Bristol young protestors who were aware of that city's historical role in the Atlantic Slave Trade pulled down a statue of Edward Colston, a seventeenth-century slave trader. Colston had been Deputy Governor of the Royal African Company. In that role Colson had been partially responsible for the enslavement and deaths of tens of thousands of Africans, yet his statue had still stood in the centre of Bristol for 125 years. After it was topped from its pedestal by protestors, the statue was dragged through the streets of Bristol and dumped into Bristol Harbour.

'Conclusion'

Cranford
Elizabeth Cleghorn Gaskell

In an English town, a group of women navigate their social relationships. In this section, Miss Betty Barker arranges a tea party for her friends. Miss Betty Barker's selection process for who is allowed at the tea party reveals the politics of their social interactions and hierarchies.

And now Miss Betty Barker had called to invite Miss Matty to tea at her house on the following Tuesday. She gave me also an impromptu invitation, as I happened to be a visitor – though I could see she had a little fear lest, since my father had gone to live in Drumble, he might have engaged in that 'horrid cotton trade,' and so dragged his family down out of 'aristocratic society.' She prefaced this invitation with so many apologies that she quite excited my curiosity. 'Her presumption' was to be excused. What had she been doing? She seemed so overpowered by it, I could only think that she had been writing to Queen Adelaide to ask for a receipt for washing lace; but the act which she so characterised was only an invitation she had carried to her sister's former mistress, Mrs Jamieson. 'Her former occupation considered, could Miss Matty excuse the liberty?' Ah! thought I, she has found out that double cap, and is going to rectify Miss Matty's head-dress. No! it was simply to extend her invitation to Miss Matty and to me. Miss Matty bowed acceptance; and I wondered that, in the graceful action, she did not feel the unusual weight and extraordinary height of her head-dress. But I do not think she did, for she recovered her balance, and went on talking to Miss Betty in a kind, condescending manner, very different from the fidgety way she would have had if she had suspected how singular her appearance was.

'Mrs Jamieson is coming, I think you said?' asked Miss Matty.

'Yes. Mrs Jamieson most kindly and condescendingly said she would be happy to come. One little stipulation she made, that she should bring Carlo. I told her that if I had a weakness, it was for dogs.'

'And Miss Pole?' questioned Miss Matty, who was thinking of her pool at Preference, in which Carlo would not be available as a partner.

'I am going to ask Miss Pole. Of course, I could not think of asking her until I had asked you, madam – the rector's daughter, madam. Believe me, I do not forget the situation my father held under yours.'

'And Mrs Forrester, of course?'

'And Mrs Forrester. I thought, in fact, of going to her before I went to Miss Pole. Although her circumstances are changed, madam, she was born a Tyrrell, and we can never forget her alliance to the Bigges, of Bigelow Hall.'

Miss Matty cared much more for the little circumstance of her being a very good card-player.

'Mrs Fitz-Adam – I suppose –'

'No, madam. I must draw a line somewhere. Mrs Jamieson would not, I think, like to meet Mrs Fitz-Adam. I have the greatest respect for Mrs Fitz-Adam – but I cannot think her fit society for such ladies as Mrs Jamieson and Miss Matilda Jenkyns.'

Miss Betty Barker bowed low to Miss Matty, and pursed up her mouth. She looked at me with sidelong dignity, as much as to say, although a retired milliner, she was no democrat, and understood the difference of ranks.

Chapter 7, 'Visiting'

Level 3 Speaking Verse and Prose: Grade 8 – Verse

Edward Hopper and the House by the Railroad

Edward Hirsch

This poem presents an artist observing a personified house.

Out here in the exact middle of the day,
This strange, gawky house has the expression
Of someone being stared at, someone holding
His breath underwater, hushed and expectant;

This house is ashamed of itself, ashamed
Of its fantastic mansard rooftop
And its pseudo-Gothic porch, ashamed
Of its shoulders and large, awkward hands.

But the man behind the easel is relentless;
He is as brutal as sunlight, and believes
The house must have done something horrible
To the people who once lived here

Because now it is so desperately empty,
It must have done something to the sky
Because the sky, too, is utterly vacant
And devoid of meaning. There are no

Trees or shrubs anywhere – the house
Must have done something against the earth.
All that is present is a single pair of tracks
Straightening into the distance. No trains pass.

Now the stranger returns to this place daily
Until the house begins to suspect
That the man, too, is desolate, desolate
And even ashamed. Soon the house starts

To stare frankly at the man. And somehow
The empty white canvas slowly takes on
The expression of someone who is unnerved,
Someone holding his breath underwater.

And then one day the man simply disappears.
He is a last afternoon shadow moving
Across the tracks, making its way
Through the vast, darkening fields.

This man will paint other abandoned mansions,
And faded cafeteria windows, and poorly lettered
Storefronts on the edges of small towns.
Always they will have this same expression,

The utterly naked look of someone
Being stared at, someone American and gawky.
Someone who is about to be left alone
Again, and can no longer stand it.

The Flowers of the Forest

Jean Elliot

This traditional Scottish poem laments the loss of soldiers at the Battle of Flodden Field.

I've heard them lilting at our ewe-milking,
Lasses a-lilting before the dawn of day;
But now they are moaning on ilka green loaning –
The Flowers of the Forest are a' wede away.

At bughts, in the morning, nae blythe lads are scorning,
The lasses are lonely, and dowie, and wae;
Nae daffin', nae gabbin', but sighing and sabbing,
Ilk ane lifts her leglin and hies her away.

In har'st, at the shearing, nae youths now are jeering,
Bandsters are lyart, and runkled, and gray;
At fair or at preaching, nae wooing nae fleeching –
The Flowers of the Forest are a' wede away.

At e'en, in the gloaming, nae younkers are roaming
'Bout stacks wi' the lasses at bogle to play;
But ilk ane sits drearie, lamenting her dearie –
The Flowers of the Forest are weded away.

Dool and wae for the order sent our lads to the Border!
The English, for ance, by guile wan the day;
The Flowers of the Forest, that fought aye the foremost,
The prime of our land, are cauld in the clay.

We'll hear nae mair lilting at our ewe-milking;
Women and bairns are heartless and wae;
Sighing and moaning on ilka green loaning –
The Flowers of the Forest are a' wede away.

Sing with Me and do not Die of Thirst

Theresa Lola

Exploring Alzheimer's, this poem foregrounds the sacred moments of love in times of change.

Alzheimer's patients sing every lyric to their favourite songs,
and this casual act becomes a dance with defiance.
Research shows our memory of music remains intact,
like the clothes of a missing child kept by a mother;
the brain stores music in a different place,
– a subtle precaution.

My grandmother bathes my grandfather
and lyrics spill from his mouth
like water from a drowned child.
He sings Johnny Nash's 'I Can See Clearly Now'
in a bass so sharp it cuts the water in half
to form a space my grandmother can walk through.
He saw water: his brain's automatic response was
to regurgitate a song that had the word 'rain' in it.
My grandmother takes in his voice and her skin splits open like an overstuffed suitcase.
My God, it must hurt for someone you love
to remember a song in clearer detail than your face.

She wonders how he knows to accentuate *blue ska-yeee-aies.*
Proof that music muscle memory
can stretch more than shaki meat.
My grandmother joins in to harmonise,
the Bible says two shall become one voice and live till
death cracks the voice in half; I paraphrased out of anger.
Her voice is shaky as waist beads on a Fela Kuti back-up dancer,
grief tugs on your vocal chords like heavy braids,
leaves it with sore and thinning edges.

As they harmonise my grandmother morphs into the song,
wipes water from her husband's face, sings
I can see clearly now the rain is gone,
and once again they are two vivacious youths
whirling through a garden in summer.
He says 'you look like the girl Mona I danced with'
and the water in the bathtub levitates to become rain.

Keep A-Pluggin' Away

Paul Laurence Dunbar

This Speaker expresses their favourite motto, which is one of resilience and ambition.

I've a humble little motto
That is homely, though it's true, –
   Keep a-pluggin' away.
It's a thing when I've an object
That I always try to do, –
   Keep a-pluggin' away.
When you've rising storms to quell,
When opposing waters swell,
It will never fail to tell, –
   Keep a-pluggin' away.

If the hills are high before
And the paths are hard to climb,
   Keep a-pluggin' away.
And remember that successes
Come to him who bides his time, –
   Keep a-pluggin' away.
From the greatest to the least,
None are from the rule released.
Be thou toiler, poet, priest,
   Keep a-pluggin' away.

Delve away beneath the surface,
There is treasure farther down, –
   Keep a-pluggin' away.
Let the rain come down in torrents,
Let the threat'ning heavens frown,
   Keep a-pluggin' away.
When the clouds have rolled away,
There will come a brighter day
All your labor to repay, –
   Keep a-pluggin' away.

There'll be lots of sneers to swallow.
There'll be lots of pain to bear, –

    Keep a-pluggin' away.
If you've got your eye on heaven,
Some bright day you'll wake up there,
    Keep a-pluggin' away.
Perseverance still is king;
Time its sure reward will bring;
Work and wait unwearying, –
    Keep a-pluggin' away.

A Green Land Full of Rivers

Sabrina Mahfouz

This poem explores family stories, relationships and histories.

A green land full of rivers
and warm-to-the-touch rain,
my Grandad said the drops washed away the pain
your legs used to feel after mama give you a lickin',
but even the ocean couldn't soothe the sting
of papa's cruel words, he knew just how to pick them.

Shipped over from Madeira to work sugar fields,
once his dad saw his mum,
he knew his fate was sealed.
She was of the forest, he was of the sea –
but in Guyana, it'd be okay, and it was.
They got married on a steamy,
sticky jungle day in May.

Him and his Chinese friend set up
the best Roti stall in town,
it did so well that once a month
he brought his wife a sparkly gown.
All the women would cut their eyes
and look and stare,
shouting at their man –
why ya kna buy me dat, I want dat, it no fair!

So the women danced with her man,
jealous for what she had,
and he was no better, dancing right back.
Frustrated by feeling inferior,
she took it out on my Grandad.
Locked him alone for days in a dark room,
with just a thin stick of sugar cane,
my Grandad prayed for her to be happy,
but the day never came.

His father spoke of England –
it was rich and grand and fair,

he spoke of it with deep-felt love –
though he'd never, ever been there.
At the age of eighteen,
Grandad buried his father and boarded a ship,
he was going to England
with just a sugar cane stick in his pocket –

it would be a long trip.

From **The Lotos-Eaters**

Alfred, Lord Tennyson

In this poem, a group of sailors land upon an enchanting and magical island.

'Courage!' he said, and pointed toward the land,
'This mounting wave will roll us shoreward soon.'
In the afternoon they came unto a land,
In which it seemed always afternoon.
All round the coast the languid air did swoon,
Breathing like one that hath a weary dream.
Full-faced above the valley stood the moon;
And like a downward smoke, the slender stream
Along the cliff to fall and pause and fall did seem.

A land of streams! some, like a downward smoke,
Slow-dropping veils of thinnest lawn, did go;
And some thro' wavering lights and shadows broke,
Rolling a slumbrous sheet of foam below.
They saw the gleaming river seaward flow
From the inner land: far off, three mountain-tops,
Three silent pinnacles of aged snow,
Stood sunset-flush'd: and, dew'd with showery drops,
Up-clomb the shadowy pine above the woven copse.

The charmed sunset linger'd low adown
In the red West: thro' mountain clefts the dale
Was seen far inland, and the yellow down
Border'd with palm, and many a winding vale
And meadow, set with slender galingale;
A land where all things always seem'd the same!
And round about the keel with faces pale,
Dark faces pale against that rosy flame,
The mild-eyed melancholy Lotos-eaters came.

Branches they bore of that enchanted stem,
Laden with flower and fruit, whereof they gave
To each, but whoso did receive of them,
And taste, to him the gushing of the wave
Far far away did seem to mourn and rave
On alien shores; and if his fellow spake,

His voice was thin, as voices from the grave;
And deep-asleep he seem'd, yet all awake,
And music in his ears his beating heart did make.

Air and Angels

John Donne

This poem explores the divine nature of love.

Twice or thrice had I lov'd thee,
Before I knew thy face or name;
So in a voice, so in a shapeless flame
Angels affect us oft, and worshipp'd be;
      Still when, to where thou wert, I came,
Some lovely glorious nothing I did see.
      But since my soul, whose child love is,
Takes limbs of flesh, and else could nothing do,
      More subtle than the parent is
Love must not be, but take a body too;
      And therefore what thou wert, and who,
        I bid Love ask, and now
That it assume thy body, I allow,
And fix itself in thy lip, eye, and brow.

Whilst thus to ballast love I thought,
And so more steadily to have gone,
With wares which would sink admiration,
I saw I had love's pinnace overfraught;
      Ev'ry thy hair for love to work upon
Is much too much, some fitter must be sought;
      For, nor in nothing, nor in things
Extreme, and scatt'ring bright, can love inhere;
      Then, as an angel, face, and wings
Of air, not pure as it, yet pure, doth wear,
      So thy love may be my love's sphere;
        Just such disparity
As is 'twixt air and angels' purity,
'Twixt women's love, and men's will ever be.

Phenomenal Woman

Maya Angelou

This poem celebrates a woman's individuality, encouraging and empowering self-confidence.

Pretty women wonder where my secret lies.
I'm not cute or built to suit a fashion model's size
But when I start to tell them,
They think I'm telling lies.
I say,
It's in the reach of my arms,
The span of my hips,
The stride of my step,
The curl of my lips.
I'm a woman
Phenomenally.
Phenomenal woman,
That's me.

I walk into a room
Just as cool as you please,
And to a man,
The fellows stand or
Fall down on their knees.
Then they swarm around me,
A hive of honey bees.
I say,
It's the fire in my eyes,
And the flash of my teeth,
The swing in my waist,
And the joy in my feet.
I'm a woman
Phenomenally.
Phenomenal woman,
That's me.

Men themselves have wondered
What they see in me.

They try so much
But they can't touch
My inner mystery.
When I try to show them,
They say they still can't see.
I say,
It's in the arch of my back,
The sun of my smile,
The ride of my breasts,
The grace of my style.
I'm a woman
Phenomenally.
Phenomenal woman,
That's me.

Now you understand
Just why my head's not bowed.
I don't shout or jump about
Or have to talk real loud.
When you see me passing,
It ought to make you proud.
I say,
It's in the click of my heels,
The bend of my hair,
the palm of my hand,
The need for my care.
'Cause I'm a woman
Phenomenally.
Phenomenal woman,
That's me.

Level 3 Speaking Verse and Prose: Grade 8 – Prose

Girl, Woman, Other
Bernardine Evaristo

Morgan, who was born Megan, identifies as gender-free. As Morgan grows up, gender stereotypes are forced upon them by their parents, especially their mother. In this section, Morgan reflects on their childhood.

wearing trousers really shouldn't have been an issue for a girl born in her time, but her mother wanted her to look cuter than she already was

like the cutest of all the cutest cutie-pies

she was determined to dress Megan up for the approval of society at large, usually other females who commented on her looks from as early as she can remember

it was the defining aspect of Megan's early childhood, she didn't actually have to do or say anything to be cute – an end in itself

which reflected well on Mum, who could bask in the glory of the compliments that poured forth as a validation of her love of an African man

between them they'd produced such an admired kid

and made the world a better place

Megan should have been grateful and accepted her cute status, what girl doesn't want to be told how lovely she is, how special?

except it felt wrong, even at a young age, something in her realized that her prettiness was supposed to make her compliant, and when she wasn't, when she rebelled, she was letting down all those invested in her being adorable

Mum being her primary cute investor

who she let down a lot, one Sunday Megan threw herself on to the floor in hysterics when forced to wear another vile, pink, puffed-up dress

and she kept it up until her mother was vanquished

Megan was her otherwise liberal mother's blind spot

there's something not quite right about Megan, she overheard her telling Aunty Sue one Sunday after lunch

as they sat drinking tea in the sitting room with just enough space for one small sofa, two armchairs and a telly

she's such a beautiful child but there's not a feminine bone in her body I hope she grows out of it, I worry about her

where will it end?

meanwhile

Dad was in the garage with Uncle Rodger, her two boy cousins, and brother Mark, tinkering with the prehistoric Cortina Dad still drove

Dad came from Malawi where he boasted everything was repairable: watches, pens, furniture, clothes, lamps, broken crockery superglued together jigsaw-style, and yes, his daughter

he was her mother's enforcer, and after the dress protest that day (victoriously, she got to wear red jeans), he'd ordered her upstairs to play with her Barbies

the Barbies with their stick legs and rocket breasts were another problem Megan had to endure

she was supposed to spend hours dressing up or playing house with them, including the darker ones she was supposed to find more relatable

in a fit she'd once tried to commit Barbicide, defaced them with coloured marker pens, chopped off hair, extracted eyes with scissors and de-limbed a few

it resulted in the punishment of bed without any tea

Chapter 4, 'Megan/Morgan'

Nineteen Eighty-Four

George Orwell

Winston lives in an imagined future. Great Britain no longer exists: it is now part of the totalitarian state Oceania, under the dictatorial control of Big Brother. Winston works for the Ministry of Truth but secretly hates Big Brother's governance. Winston keeps a diary – a crime in the thought policing world – and addresses it to O'Brien, who he thinks is part of the Brotherhood working to overthrow the Party.

He wondered, as he had many times wondered before, whether he himself was a lunatic. Perhaps a lunatic was simply a minority of one. At one time it had been a sign of madness to believe that the earth goes round the sun; today, to believe that the past is unalterable. He might be ALONE in holding that belief, and if alone, then a lunatic. But the thought of being a lunatic did not greatly trouble him: the horror was that he might also be wrong.

He picked up the children's history book and looked at the portrait of Big Brother which formed its frontispiece. The hypnotic eyes gazed into his own. It was as though some huge force were pressing down upon you – something that penetrated inside your skull, battering against your brain, frightening you out of your beliefs, persuading you, almost, to deny the evidence of your senses. In the end the Party would announce that two and two made five, and you would have to believe it. It was inevitable that they should make that claim sooner or later: the logic of their position demanded it. Not merely the validity of experience, but the very existence of external reality, was tacitly denied by their philosophy. The heresy of heresies was common sense. And what was terrifying was not that they would kill you for thinking otherwise, but that they might be right. For, after all, how do we know that two and two make four? Or that the force of gravity works? Or that the past is unchangeable? If both the past and the external world exist only in the mind, and if the mind itself is controllable what then?

But no! His courage seemed suddenly to stiffen of its own accord. The face of O'Brien, not called up by any obvious association, had floated into his mind. He knew, with more certainty than before, that O'Brien was on his side. He was writing the diary for O'Brien – TO O'Brien: it was like an interminable letter which no one would ever read, but which was addressed to a particular person and took its colour from that fact.

The Party told you to reject the evidence of your eyes and ears. It was their final, most essential command. His heart sank as he thought of the enormous power arrayed against him, the ease with which any Party intellectual would overthrow him in debate, the subtle arguments which he would not be able to understand, much less answer. And yet he was in the right! They were wrong and he was right. The obvious, the silly, and the true had got to be defended. Truisms are true, hold on to that! The solid world exists, its laws do not change. Stones are hard, water is wet, objects unsupported fall towards the earth's centre. With the feeling that he was speaking to O'Brien, and also that he was setting forth an important axiom, he wrote:

Freedom is the freedom to say that two plus two make four. If that is granted, all else follows.

Chapter 7

Sula

Toni Morrison

Nel Wright and Sula Peace live in the Bottom, a neighbourhood on a hill near the fictional town of Medallion, Ohio. In their youth, Nel and Sula are best friends. This section explores their close friendship.

They were solitary little girls whose loneliness was so profound it intoxicated them and sent them stumbling into Technicolored visions that always included a presence, a someone, who, quite like the dreamer, shared the delight of the dream. When Nel, an only child, sat on the steps of her back porch surrounded by the high silence of her mother's incredibly orderly house, feeling the neatness pointing at her back, she studied the poplars and fell easily into a picture of herself lying on a flowered bed, tangled in her own hair, waiting for some fiery prince. He approached but never quite arrived. But always, watching the dream along with her, were some smiling sympathetic eyes. Someone as interested as she herself in the flow of her imagined hair, the thickness of the mattress of flowers, the voile sleeves that closed below her elbows in gold-threaded cuffs.

Similarly, Sula, also an only child, but wedged into a household of throbbing disorder constantly awry with things, people, voices and the slamming of doors, spent hours in the attic behind a roll of linoleum galloping through her own mind on a gray-and-white horse tasting sugar and smelling roses in full view of a someone who shared both the taste and the speed.

So when they met, first in those chocolate halls and next through the ropes of the swing, they felt the ease and comfort of old friends. Because each had discovered years before that they were neither white nor male, and that all freedom and triumph was forbidden to them, they had set about creating something else to be. Their meeting was fortunate, for it let them use each other to grow on. Daughters of distant mothers and incomprehensible fathers (Sula's because he was dead; Nel's because he wasn't), they found in each other's eyes the intimacy they were looking for.

Nel Wright and Sula Peace were both twelve in 1922, wishbone thin and easy-assed. Nel was the color of wet sandpaper – just dark enough to escape the blows of the pitch-black truebloods and the contempt of old women who worried about things such as bad blood mixtures and knew that the origins of a mule and mulatto were one and the same. Had she been any lighter-skinned

she would have needed either her mother's protection on the way to school or a streak of mean to defend herself. Sula was a heavy brown with large quiet eyes, one of which featured a birthmark that spread from the middle of the lid toward the eyebrow, shaped something like a stemmed rose. It gave her otherwise plain face a broken excitement and blue-blade threat like the keloid scar of the razored man who sometimes played checkers with her grandmother. The birthmark was to grow darker as the years passed, but now it was the same shade as her gold-flecked eyes, which, to the end, were as steady and clean as rain.

Their friendship was as intense as it was sudden.

'1922'

A Sentimental Journey Through France and Italy

Laurence Sterne

Yorick is travelling through France. Yorick has recently been informed that the French police are looking for him because he does not have a passport. Here, Yorick tries to rationalise his potential imprisonment, but upon seeing a caged starling, his opinions change.

– And as for the Bastile; the terror is in the word. – Make the most of it you can, said I to myself, the Bastile is but another word for tower; – and a tower is but another word for a house you can't get out of. – Mercy on the gouty! for they are in it twice a year. – But with nine livres a day, a pen and ink, and paper, and patience, albeit a man can't get out, he may do very well within, – at least for a month or six weeks; at the end of which, if he is a harmless fellow his innocence appears, and he comes out a better and wiser man than he went in.

I had some occasion (I forget what) to step into the court-yard, as I settled this account; and remember I walk'd down stairs in no small triumph with the conceit of my reasoning. – Beshrew the sombre pencil! said I, vauntingly – for I envy not its powers, which paints the evils of life with so hard and deadly a colouring. The mind sits terrified at the objects she has magnified herself, and blackened: reduce them to their proper size and hue, she overlooks them. – 'Tis true, said I, correcting the proposition, – the Bastile is not an evil to be despised; – but strip it of its towers, fill up the fosse, – unbarricade the doors – call it simply a confinement, and suppose 'tis some tyrant of a distemper – and not of a man which holds you in it – the evil half vanishes, and you bear the other half without complaint.

I was interrupted in the hey-day of this soliloquy, with a voice which I took to be of a child, which complained 'it could not get out.' – I look'd up and down from the passage, and seeing neither man, woman, or child, I went out without further attention.

In my return back through the passage, I heard the same words repeated twice over; and looking up, I saw it was a starling hung in a little cage. – 'I can't get out – I can't get out,' said the starling.

I stood looking at the bird: and to every person who came through the passage it ran fluttering to the side towards which they approach'd it, with the same lamentation of its captivity. 'I can't get out', said the starling – God help thee! said I, but I'll let thee out, cost what it will; so I turned about the cage to get

to the door; it was twisted and double twisted so fast with wire, there was no getting it open without pulling the cage to pieces. – I took both hands to it.

The bird flew to the place where I was attempting his deliverance, and thrusting his head through the trellis, pressed his breast against it as if impatient. – I fear, poor creature! said I, I cannot set thee at liberty. – 'No,' said the starling, – 'I can't get out – I can't get out,' said the starling.

I vow I never had my affections more tenderly awakened.

'The Passport: The Hotel at Paris'

Hamnet
Maggie O'Farrell

Set in Stratford in the late 1500s, Hamnet is the son of the soon to be famous playwright William Shakespeare. At home, Hamnet's twin sister Judith has grown very unwell. Distressed by the risk to Judith's life, Hamnet decides to trick Death by swapping places with his sister. In this section, Hamnet executes his plan.

Then the idea strikes him. He doesn't know why he hadn't thought of it before. It occurs to Hamnet, as he crouches there, next to her, that it might be possible to hoodwink Death, to pull off the trick he and Judith have been playing on people since they were young: to exchange places and clothes, leading people to believe that each was the other. Their faces are the same. People remark on this all the time, at least once a day. All it takes is for Hamnet to put on Judith's shawl or for her to don his hat; they will sit at the table like that, eyes lowered, smiles concealed, and their mother will place a hand on Judith's shoulder and say, Hamnet, can you bring in the wood? Or their father might come into a room and see what he thinks is his son, dressed in a jerkin, and ask him to conjugate a verb in Latin, only to discover it is his daughter, hiding her laughter, revelling in the illusion, and she will push aside the door to reveal the real son, hidden away.

Could he pull off their trick, their joke, just once more? He thinks he can. He thinks he will. He glances over his shoulder at the tunnel of dark beside the door. The blackness is depthless, soft, absolute. Turn away, he says to Death. Close your eyes. Just for a moment.

He slides his hands underneath Judith, one palm under her shoulders, the other under her hips, and he shunts her sideways, towards the fireplace. She is lighter than he expected; she rolls to her side and her eyes open a crack as she rights herself. She watches, frowning, as he lays himself down in the dip her body has made, as he takes her place, as he smooths his hair down, on either side of his face, as he pulls the sheet up over both of them, tucking it under their chins.

They will look, he is sure, the same. No one will know which is which. It will be easy for Death to make a mistake, to take him in her place.

She is stirring beside him, trying to sit up. 'Nay,' she is saying again. 'Hamnet, nay.'

He knew she would know straight away what he was doing. She always does. She is shaking her head, but is too weak to raise herself from the pallet.

Hamnet holds the sheet fast over both of them.

He breathes in. He breathes out. He turns his head and breathes into the whorls of her ear; he breathes in his strength, his health, his all. You will stay, is what he whispers, and I will go. He sends these words into her: I want you to take my life. It shall be yours. I give it to you.

They cannot both live: he sees this and she sees this. There is not enough life, enough air, enough blood for both of them. Perhaps there never was. And if either of them is to live, it must be her.

What Strange Paradise

Omar El Akkad

Amir is a nine-year-old Syrian boy fleeing his homeland in search of safety. He crosses the Mediterranean in an unstable, unsafe boat along with other refugees. In this section, the boat capsizes under the weight of so many passengers.

Amir held on to a rusted cleat on the deck, struggling to keep from sliding portside as wave after wave smashed into the hull behind him. Dexterous claws leapt upward, over the gunwale and down onto the deck, the water digging into the rot-green flesh of the *Calypso*. With every wave the boat tipped father onto its side, the passengers skittering sideways, the critical angle closing in, after which the vessel would continue its rotation, capsizing.

A deep cracking sound emerged from somewhere below, the hull giving way. As the *Calypso* tilted, the flashlight came loose from its hook and was washed overboard. Only the faint backlit clouds and the distant colored lights of shore provided illumination. The passengers screamed and shouted for help, their voices no sooner escaping the boat than they were swallowed by the storm. To anyone standing at the shore the *Calypso* would have been just another parcel of nighttime, unheard and unseen.

Another man pushed his way through the crowd and onto the portside railing. He zipped his orange life vest as high as it would go and then, stumbling as though punch-drunk, he tried to step onto the railing, preparing to dive in pursuit of the Tunisian who moments earlier had made a break for the shore. He managed one foot up before the boat shuddered violently and tilted, throwing him overboard. He tumbled, colliding neck-first with the water, and whether it was the sea or the night that took him, in an instant he vanished from view.

'Stay on the boat, damn you, stay on the boat,' Mohamed shouted. 'Whoever jumps dies.' But as the waves increased in ferocity, washing the deck entirely and shattering the remaining wheelhouse windows, more and more passengers leapt overboard. The ones who'd brought life vests from the smugglers went first, struggling for traction on the sea-slick deck, orienting themselves in the direction of the music and the colored lights. Each after the other in rag-doll posture, they took flight, each after the other they disappeared, the floating world rising up to meet them.

Among those readying to jump, Amir saw Umm Ibrahim. In the bedlam she'd moved portside, the kneeling side that dipped with every wave until it neared touching the water. Amir watched her as she steadied herself against a fellow passenger, and then in one motion reached down and pulled her niqab completely off.

Underneath she wore a bright, sleeveless summer dress, decorated with watercolour lilacs. An orange life jacket rested too high on her frame, pushed upward by the rise of her belly. As she stood at the edge, she turned and scanned the deck. The boat righted itself with a falling thud between waves, and the water drained away. There came over the *Calypso* a kind of diastolic silence, a temporary pause. And in this pause Amir and Umm Ibrahim caught eyes.

'Come back,' Amir yelled. 'Don't go, don't go.'

Umm Ibrahim looked at the boy as though she'd never seen him before. She turned and, the boat rising and tilting in her direction, jumped.

Chapter 26, 'Before'

To the Lighthouse
Virginia Woolf

*The Ramsay family live in a summer house off the coast of Scotland. Lily Briscoe
is a young painter who is attempting to paint a portrait of Mrs Ramsay and
her son James. She is haunted her inability to create art. In this section, she
attempts to overcome this insecurity.*

Where to begin? – that was the question; at what point to make the first mark?
One line placed on the canvas committed her to innumerable risks, to frequent
and irrevocable decisions. All that in idea seemed simple became in practice
immediately complex; as the waves shape themselves symmetrically from
the cliff top, but to the swimmer among them are divided by steep gulfs, and
foaming crests. Still the risk must be run; the mark made.

With a curious physical sensation, as if she were urged forward and at the
same time must hold herself back, she made her first quick decisive stroke.
The brush descended. It flickered brown over the white canvas; it left a running
mark. A second time she did it – a third time. And so pausing and so flickering,
she attained a dancing rhythmical movement, as if the pauses were one part
of the rhythm and the strokes another, and all were related; and so, lightly and
swiftly pausing, striking, she scored her canvas with brown running nervous
lines which had no sooner settled there than they enclosed (she felt it looming
out at her) a space. Down in the hollow of her wave she saw the next wave
towering higher and higher above her. For what could be more formidable than
that space? Here she was again, she thought, stepping back to look at it, drawn
out of gossip, out of living, out of community with people into the presence of
this formidable ancient enemy of hers – this other thing, this truth, this reality,
which suddenly laid hands on her, emerged stark at the back of appearances
and commanded her attention. She was half unwilling, half reluctant. Why
always be drawn out and haled away? Why not left in peace, to talk to Mr
Carmichael on the lawn? It was an exacting form of intercourse anyhow. Other
worshipful objects were content with worship; men, women, God, all let one
kneel prostrate; but this form, were it only the shape of a white lamp-shade
looming on a wicker table, roused on to perpetual combat, challenged one to
fight in which one was bound to be worsted. Always (it was in her nature, or
in her sex, she did not know which) before she exchanged the fluidity of life
for the concentration of painting she had a few moments of nakedness when
she seemed like an unborn soul, a soul reft of body, hesitating on some windy
pinnacle and exposed without protection to all the blasts of doubt. Why then

did she do it? She looked at the canvas, lightly scored with running lines. It would be hung in the servants' bedrooms. It would be rolled up and stuffed under a sofa. What was the good of doing it then, and she heard some voice saying she couldn't paint, saying she couldn't create, as if she were caught up in one of those habitual currents in which after a certain time experience forms in the mind, so that one repeats words without being aware any longer who originally spoke them.

Can't paint, can't write, she murmured monotonously, anxiously considering what her plan of attack should be.

Part 3, 'The Lighthouse'; Chapter 3

Circe
Madeline Miller

Circe is the divine daughter of Helios and Perse. After discovering Circe's power for witchcraft, the Gods banish her from the house of Helios. She is forced to live in exile on the island of Aiaia. In this section, Circe discovers her affinity for collecting wild herbs and flowers.

I stepped into those woods and my life began.

I learnt to plait my hair back, so it would not catch on every twig, and how to tie my skirts at the knee to keep the burrs off. I learned to recognise the different blooming vines and gaudy roses, to spot the shining dragonflies and coiling snakes. I climbed the peaks where the cypresses speared black into the sky, then clambered down to the orchards and vineyards where purple grapes grew thick as coral. I walked the hills, the buzzing meadows of thyme and lilac, and set my footprints across the yellow beaches. I searched out every cove and grotto, found the gentle bays, the harbour safe for ships. I heard the wolves howl, and the frogs cry from their mud. I stroked the glossy brown scorpions who braved me with their tails. Their poison was barely a pinch. I was drunk, as the wine and nectar in my father's halls had never made me. No wonder I have been so slow, I thought. All this while I have been a weaver without wool, a ship without sea. Yet now look where I sail.

At night I went home to my house. I did not mind its shadows anymore, for they meant my father's gaze was gone from the sky and the hours were my own. I did not mind the emptiness either. For a thousand years I had tried to fill the space between myself and my family; filling the rooms of my house was easy by comparison. I burned cedar in the fireplace, and its dark smoke kept me company. I sang, which had never been allowed before, since my mother said I had the voice of a drowning gull. And when I did get lonely, when I found myself yearning for my brother, or Glaucos as he had been, then there was always the forest. The lizards darted along the branches, the birds flashed their wings. The flowers, when they saw me, seemed to press forward like eager puppies, leaping and clamouring for my touch. I felt almost shy of them, but day by day I grew bolder, and at last I knelt in the damp earth before a clump of hellebore.

The delicate blooms fluttered on their stalks. I did not need a knife to cut them, only the edge of my nail, which grew sticky with flecks of sap. I put the flowers in a basket covered with cloth and only uncovered them when I was home

again, my shutters firmly closed. I did not think anyone would try to stop me, but I did not intend to tempt them to it.

I looked at the blossoms lying on my table. They seemed shrunken, etiolated. I did not have the first idea of what I should do to them. Chop? Boil? Roast? There had been oil in my brother's ointment, but I did not know what kind. Would olive from the kitchen work? Surely not. It must be something fantastical, like seed-oil pressed from the fruits of the Hesperides. But I could not get that. I rolled a stalk beneath my finger. It turned over, limp as a drowned worm.

Well, I said to myself, do not just stand there like a stone. Try something. Boil them. Why not?

Chapter 7

Title Index

Author Index

Copyright and Acknowledgements

is There to Know about Love? © Brian Bilston. Reproduced by permission of Jo Unwin Literary Agency.

Birch, Beverley, *Song Beneath the Tides* © 2020 Beverley Birch. Reproduced by permission of Guppy Books.

Black, Sheila, *What You Mourn* from *House of Bone* © 2006 WordTech Communications LLC Cincinnati, Ohio, USA. Reproduced by permission of WordTech Communications LLC Cincinnati.

Blackman, Malorie, *Boys Don't Cry* published by Doubleday Childrens © Oneta Malorie Blackman 2010. Reproduced by permission of Penguin Books Limited and The Agency (London) Ltd.

Blackman, Malorie, *Contact* © 2017 Malorie Blackman. Reproduced by permission of HarperCollins Publishers Ltd.

Bloom, Valerie, *Seasons* from *Hot Like Fire and Other Poems* (Bloomsbury) and *Dis Breeze* from *Let Me Touch the Sky* (Macmillan) © 2000 Valerie Bloom. Reproduced by permission of Eddison Pearson Ltd on behalf of Valerie Bloom.

Brankin, Emma, *Attention Seekers* © 2023 Emma Brankin. Reproduced by permission of the author.

Burton, Jessie, *Medusa* © Jessie Burton 2021, *Medusa*, Bloomsbury Publishing Plc. Reproduced by permission of Bloomsbury Publishing Plc.

Canfield, John, *He Thinks of his Past Faces* from *Poetry for a Change* © 2018 John Canfield. Reproduced by permission of Otter Barry Books.

Charters, Kirsten, *Something About That Day* © 2024 Kirsten Charters. Reproduced by permission of the author.

Coelho, Joseph, *The Slime Takeover, The Shockadile Crocodile!,* and *Say How You Feel,* from *Poems Aloud,* written by Joseph Coelho and illustrated by Daniel Gray-Barnett, published by Wide Eyed Editions, an imprint of The Quarto Group, copyright © 2020. Reproduced by permission of Quarto Publishing Plc.

Coelho, Joseph, *The Laugh* and *A Tip of the Slongue,* from *Smile Out Loud,* written by Joseph Coelho and illustrated by Daniel Gray-Barnett, published by Wide Eyed Editions, an imprint of The Quarto Group, copyright © 2022. Reproduced by permission of Quarto Publishing Plc.

Shamsie, Kamila, *Home Fire* © 2017 Kamila Shamsie. Used by permission of Riverhead, an imprint of Penguin Publishing Group, a division of Penguin Random House LLC. All rights reserved. Copyright © Kamila Shamsie, 2017, *Home Fire*, Bloomsbury Publishing Plc. Reproduced by permission of Bloomsbury Publishing Plc.

Soundar, Chitra, *Sona Sharma, Looking After Planet Earth* © 2021 Chitra Soundar. Written by Chitra Soundar and Illustrated by Jen Khatun. Reproduced by permission of Walker Books Ltd, London, SE11 5HJ (www.walker.co.uk).

Subramaniam, Suma, *Filter* © 2021 Suma Subramaniam. Reproduced by permission of the author.

Tanikawa, Shuntarō, *Ball of Yarn* from *New Selected Poems* translated by William I. Elliott and Kazuo Kawamura © 2015 Shuntarō Tanikawa. Reproduced by permission of Carcanet Press Limited.

Teed, Nick, *Jungle Noises* © 2023 Nick Teed. Reproduced by permission of the author.

Terry, Rosa, *Home* © 2023 Rosa Terry. Reproduced by permission of the author as part of LAMDA Learners' Poetry Prize 2023.

Thomas, Angie, *The Hate U Give** © 2017 Angie Thomas. Reproduced by permission of Walker Books Ltd, London, SE11 5HJ (www.walker.co.uk). Reproduced by permission of Harper Collins Publishers.

Torday, Piers, *There May Be a Castle* © 2016 Piers Torday. Reproduced by kind permission of the author and Conville & Walsh Limited.

Toutoungi, Claudine, *Cold Toast, Bertie Beaky, What a to-do!* and *Voyage to the Bottom of my Bowl* © 2024 Claudine Toutoungi. Reproduced by permission of the author.

Uehashi, Nahoko, *The Beast Player* translated by Cathy Hirano. Text copyright © 2009 by Nahoko Uehashi. English translation copyright © 2018 by Cathy Hirano. Reprinted by permission of Henry Holt Books for Young Readers. All Rights Reserved. Reproduced by permission of Pushkin Children's Books.

Venkatraman, Padma, *Whenever you see a tree* © 2021 Padma Venkatraman. Reproduced by permission of the author.

Wakeling, Kate, *The Flibbit* © 2021 Kate Wakeling. Reproduced by permission of The Emma Press Limited.